I0548136

SPEAKING TO THE UNSEEN

A CHANTALENE MYSTERY

ALSO BY
MARCIA PRESTON

THE SPIDERLING

THE WIND COMES SWEEPING

TRUDY'S PROMISE

THE PIANO MAN

THE BUTTERFLY HOUSE

SONG OF THE BONES

PERHAPS SHE'LL DIE

SPEAKING TO THE UNSEEN

A CHANTALENE MYSTERY

MARY HIGGINS CLARK AWARD WINNER

MARCIA PRESTON

ROGUE RIVER

An Imprint of Roan & Weatherford Publishing Associates, LLC
Bentonville, Arkansas
www.roanweatherford.com

Library of Congress Cataloging-in-Publication Data
Names: Preston, Marcia, author.
Title: Speaking to the Unseen/Marcia Preston | Chantalene #3
Description: First Edition. | Bentonville: Rogue River, 2023.
Identifiers: LCCN: 2024936324 | ISBN: 978-1-63373-928-4 (hardcover) |
ISBN: 978-1-63373-929-1 (trade paperback) | ISBN: 978-1-63373-930-7 (eBook)
Subjects: | BISAC: FICTION/Mystery & Detective/Women Sleuths | FICTION/Women
FICTION/Mystery & Detective/Traditional | FICTION/Thrillers/Crime
LC record available at: https://lccn.loc.gov/2024936324

Rogue River trade paperback edition November, 2024

Cover Design by Casey W. Cowan
Interior Design & Electronic Formatting by Staci Troilo
Editing by George "Clay" Mitchell & Don Money

ACKNOWLEDGMENTS

Thanks to the good folks at Roan & Weatherford Publishing and to Linda, John, Rakell, and Inez.

ONE

TWO EVENTS SENT me into the heart of the Ozarks that October searching for the missing links in my Gypsy history. The first was a letter from Drew, the man I almost married, who was practicing law again in New York. He needed to see me. If I agreed, he would book a flight and come to Oklahoma. I was still considering whether needed to see me was the same as wanted, when the second shoe dropped.

My tests had turned up a defect of the mitochondrial chromosome. During the follow-up to a routine medical exam for health insurance, a specialist I'd never met looked at my chart with impassive eyes and told me I was going to die. The dysfunction, inherited maternally, was so rare that few statistics existed. Limited studies predicted the average life span of women with this mutation was thirty-three years.

I had just turned thirty.

There was no known treatment or cure.

The doctor began a detailed explanation, but my mind glazed over. Shock, nausea, and anger came in quick succession. Cycling around to disbelief.

My voice sounded hoarse. "I'd like a second opinion."

Doctor Dickson had rimless glasses, a bald head, and a voice like Pavarotti. "Miss Morrell," he said calmly, "I am the second opinion. Your family doctor diagnosed the problem from abnormalities in your bloodwork, and he asked me to weigh in because genetics is my specialization."

My legs went numb.

He focused on the computer monitor in the exam room. "How old was your mother when she died?"

"Thirty-two. But that doesn't count. She was murdered."

He didn't even blink. "What about your maternal grandmother?"

"I don't know. She disappeared when my mother was a baby. Mom was raised by her grandmother, so there's at least one woman in my family who lived past her thirties."

"Interesting."

I felt perfectly healthy, yet this man was delivering a death sentence with all the compassion of an executioner. I had a primal impulse to kill the messenger. The next instant I was swamped by a sorrow so deep I could hardly breathe. My poor body, betrayed by its own cells.

The doctor closed my computer file and glanced at his watch. "We'll repeat the bloodwork in six months, to see if anything's changed. Meanwhile," he met my eyes for the first time since coming into the room, "if there's anything you've always wanted to do, now would be a good time to do it." He hesitated only a moment before leaving the room.

I hit the revolving doors of the clinic like an avalanche, but they were glacially slow no matter how I pushed. Eventually the doors spit me into the afternoon sun and I strode to my car, head up, spots glittering before my eyes. I unlocked the door and threw myself inside.

I was not ready to die. A stubborn part of me refused to believe this doctor. I would get a third opinion, and everything would be fine.

———————————

HEAT POURED THROUGH the windshield but I shivered, breathing like a beached fish. My life had just been cut in half. Less than half. I'd thought I had years to live out the plot points of my story. I had never married. Had never seen Paris, Niagara Falls, or the Grand Canyon. Never had a child. A longing like homesickness tightened my chest. I missed all those places I'd never been, and the people I might meet. I missed me.

I had known life wasn't fair since I was twelve years old and lost both my parents. But, thus inoculated, I believed I was immune. My share of tragedy came early in life. Fate owed me a lucky future. What a moron.

What if my life was over in three years—or less? This could not be happening.

I'm not a crier but I wanted to howl. I forced a deep breath and opened my eyes. In the parking lot, people were coming and going as if the world hadn't changed. As if they had whole lifetimes to work out their loves and losses and dreams.

Yesterday's mail lay on the seat beside me, Drew's opened letter on top. I picked it up and thought of his hands on the envelope, long-fingered and graceful. I imagined the way his muzzy eyebrows inched together as he wrote the words. I loved this man and let him walk away because I wasn't ready to get married. I thought I had time.

In the two years since I'd last seen Drew, my e-mail and phone number changed, but the U.S. Postal Service knew where to find me in the Oklahoma hills where I was born. The fact that Drew had written a letter by hand and sent it snail mail amazed me as much as his message. I pictured him flying to Oklahoma City, and renting a car, driving the Indian Nation turnpike to my small farm. The prospect hummed in my brain like a tuning fork. I hadn't missed him this much since the wretched weeks right after he left.

Drew and I had separated over his desire to get married and start a family immediately. He was several years older, had been through one failed marriage, and was more than ready for a settled life. I wanted a family too, eventually, and definitely with him. I had been through some major trauma surrounding the loss of my parents, and I simply wasn't ready for the kind of partnership a marriage should be.

How could I have children now, knowing I might pass down this defect to my daughter? What if I left young kids behind the way my mother and grandmother had done? Having been one of those kids, I knew how tough it was.

In the unchained history of the women in my family, there was one solid link—my great-grandmother, the Gypsy matriarch who raised my mother. I met Gamma Rose only once, when I was ten. She would be in her nineties now if she was still alive. If she had died, I wasn't sure anyone would have notified me.

As far as I knew, Gamma Rose was my only living relative. I should have tried to find her when I'd learned the details of my mother's death, more than a decade after the fact. Instead, I had written a letter. The last address I had for her was a post office box somewhere in northern Arkansas, a blip too remote to have a name on Google Earth.

If she was still living, did that disprove the doctor's prediction? What about her daughter, my grandmother, who had run away from the Gypsy life when she was young? Was she still alive? If I had two living female ancestors, perhaps the women in my family defied the mitochondrial curse. Maybe I still had time.

There was one way to find out. By ten o'clock the next morning, I was driving twisted roads through the Ozark Mountains, desperate not to be the last leaf on my family tree.

TWO

WHEN I WAS twelve years old my father was accused of raping a teenaged girl in our small country town. He was brought to trial and acquitted after three different men testified that he was playing poker with them that night. Certain townsfolk weren't convinced and a week later he was found hanged in an old barn. My mother disappeared that same night. The law declared my father's death a suicide. There was even a fake note. It was ten years before I could prove what really happened. Some of the locals still resented me for exposing the truth and wished I would leave town. It was one of the reasons I'd stayed.

Thelma Patterson was not one of those. Thelma was thirty years my senior and my best friend. She had stuck with me through my search for the truth, and I returned the favor when she needed help. We had history. The day I left the doctor's office with my death sentence, I drove straight to her house.

I sat at Thelma's kitchen table with a glass of sweet tea fogging in my hands. It was therapeutic to see Thelma's face cycle through all the emotions I'd felt an hour before. Neither of us accepted the prognosis. We were not wired that way.

She wanted details. I gave her the doctor's report with as many specifics as I could remember. "He said each cell in the body can contain thousands of mitochondria which move around converting food molecules into energy. But their DNA is distinct from the cell nucleus, which makes scientists suspect mitochondria had a past existence as separate organisms. Eventually they became interdependent and essential to their host cells. Apparently my mitochondria are staging a coup and trying to achieve independence again. The effects of the rebellion will be fatal."

It was like talking about some unlucky acquaintance, not something that was happening to me.

"Good grief, that's complicated," Thelma said, frowning. "I don't understand how that could kill you. Or why they don't have some medication to treat it."

"I don't either. I just know I want to find my great-grandmother and see if she knows what happened to my grandmother. If both of them are still living, I can believe I have a shot at beating this."

Thelma nodded, her chin set firm. "I'll keep an eye on your place and feed your animals. Take as much time as you need."

"Thanks." I had only two animals—a dog and a horse—and they both knew Thelma on sight. My income came from a job in town, not from farming, though in spring and summer I grew fresh vegetables for sale in local markets. "I'll call my boss. If she won't approve the time off, I'm going anyway."

"Don't blame you. But I know JoAnn. I think she'll understand." Thelma squeezed my hand, but let go before either of us got runny. "Are you going to tell Drew?" She knew about his letter.

"I don't know yet. If he's coming to tell me that he's found someone else and is planning to get married, there's no point."

It's exactly what he would do in that situation, make the trip to give me the news in person. He had that much integrity. By comparison, I felt like a moral wimp.

"I doubt that's his reason." Thelma looked over her glasses at me. "And so do you."

I shrugged. "Wish you could go to Arkansas with me. But there's nobody else I can trust to feed Bones and Whippoorwill."

"I know. Besides, this might be one of those things a body has to do alone." She walked me to the door. "Remember. Medicine is not an exact science."

The next morning at daylight, I scratched Bones's ears, gave Whippoorwill extra oats, and hit the road in my Honda CRV.

THE OZARKS ARE friendly and rounded with trees, like shrunken Smoky Mountains. In October the slopes were tinged with copper and gold. With my days possibly numbered, I got misty-eyed at the sight of pumpkins spilling from produce stands along sheltered roads. I always wanted to travel but couldn't afford it. The names on my Arkansas map intrigued me. Monkey Run. Possum Trot. Toad Suck.

Crooked Dog Creek, however, wasn't on the map, and the last letter I had from Gamma Rose was postmarked there. After several stops to ask questions, I found a wide spot beside two lanes of blacktop that corkscrewed into the hills. Crooked Dog Creek wasn't a town anymore, just a gnome-sized post office that the United States Postal Service would probably close after the next census.

I parked on the dusty shoulder. Across the blacktop, the eyeless remains of a store and gas station decomposed in silence. I got out and stretched my legs, looking up at tree-covered slopes that crowded in on all sides. I grew up in open spaces. A narrow sky made me uneasy. The one time I'd visited Manhattan with Drew, those concrete canyons pressed in on me like the walls of an open grave.

I took a deep breath as if air was scarce, then put my shoulder to the sticky door of the post office. White paint flaked onto my shirt, and the hinges squawked like a chicken. The interior was shadowed, cool, and smelled like a cave. I checked the ceiling. No bats, so I walked to the service window and peered inside. "Hello?"

Tiny shrunken heads were laid out on a worktable, along with various body parts. If there's anything creepier than clowns, it's apple dolls, with their rosy-cheeks and mortuary smiles. I suspect they are used for voodoo. But the postmistress, sitting in an overstuffed chair crocheting a doll dress, looked plumply benign. She didn't bother to get up but greeted me with a smile.

"How may I help you?"

I asked her if she knew Gamma Rose Tsura and where she lived.

"Everybody knows Gamma Rose. About five miles over the next mountain." She pointed. "Ten miles by car."

I'd been on the road since morning and the prospect of more snaky miles writhed in my stomach. I was extremely grateful to know my great-grandmother was alive. Thanking the doll-maker, I turned to leave.

"You won't find her home, though," she said, never missing a stitch in her handiwork.

I turned back. "Why not?"

"Gamma Rose has been in the county hospital over at Madison for two weeks." She shook her head sadly. "I doubt she'll ever come home. She's older than God's mother."

That's pretty damned old.

She eyed me curiously over half-glasses. "It's a shame she has no kin to look after her best interests."

She was fishing. I smiled, but as the old farmer who was my foster dad used to say, you can't fish a fisher. I offered no information, thanked her again and left.

The sun dropped behind the hills and cast a shady chill over the woods. I wished for a caffeinated roadie. Too bad the dilapidated store was out of business.

I skirted the town of Madison on my way here and now retraced my route. By the time my car rolled through the modest streets of the town, dusk was gathering on the shady side of the wooded hills. Blue and white signs pointed me easily to the hospital, a three-story stucco building set against a backdrop of trees along a creek. Surprisingly prime real estate for a county hospital.

My headlights flashed across the parking lot where pickups and mud-stained SUVs were scattered like a kid's jacks among the parking spaces. I sent up a fervent hope that Gamma Rose was well enough to talk to me and could remember who I was. Both seemed unlikely.

The reception desk was manned by a senior volunteer. It said so right on her name tag. I inquired about my great-grandmother and the woman consulted a list.

"She's been moved to the hospice facility next door," the volunteer said.

"Hospice?" A blade of sorrow and guilt sliced through me. I should have made this trip years ago.

She pointed toward a side exit. "Go out that door and across the breezeway. The hospice facility is privately run," she said, "and very accommodating to family and friends."

I pondered that odd description as I followed the breezeway into a flat building with hallways spanning out from the center like spokes. The air smelled like candle wax and old people's clothes. I'd never been good in hospitals and this was Hospital Xtreme.

The charge nurse lost her cheerful smile when I explained who I was. "You've come just in time." She leaned closer and lowered her voice. "This morning she was speaking to the unseen."

I didn't know what that meant and was afraid to ask. My chest felt bow-strung as I followed her directions to room twelve and pushed open the door.

From the brightly lit hallway I stepped into startling darkness. The room was over-warm. Candle flames, pale as the moon, trembled when the door breathed shut behind me. Gradually, I saw a figure pillowed in white bedding and heard the rasp of breath, ancient and tired.

I stepped closer and whispered, "Gamma Rose?"

Her eyes were closed, her mouth sunken and lipless. Was this the vigorous woman I knew from our one meeting twenty years ago? Part of me refused to believe it. I spoke her name again but got no response.

I felt their presence before I saw them—dark shapes in my peripheral vision. A sensation like spider feet ran up my back. Gamma Rose and I were not alone.

They hunched like burned stumps around the perimeter of the room, seated on chairs or pressed into corners. They were dressed in black with scarves covering their hair. I got a flickering glimpse of faces, watching me.

All women. All silent and leathered by years.

I understood why they were here. These were the old ones who kept the Romani traditions.

My mother had seldom talked of her time among the Romani. When she did, she called herself Gypsy, ignoring twentieth-century political correctness. She had defied tradition by marrying a gadžo, a non-Romani. After that, she was an outcast from her people, bolime. The stigma extended to her family and caused Gamma Rose shame. But Gamma Rose loved my mother and welcomed us when I was ten and Mom took me to meet her. To my young eyes my great-grandmother looked ancient even then, and everything about her had sparked my curiosity. There was nothing politically correct about her, either.

In her youth Gamma Rose traveled with the Zingaro caravan, living by their wits and sharp trading. She was long settled when I met her. In her house, every person had his own plate, cup, and utensils, with separate ones for guests. An old Gypsy never ate or drank from any dishes but his own. After supper, my mother and I sat with her at the kitchen table and played cards. Gamma Rose loved cards but disapproved of gambling. Unless the game was fixed in her favor, then it wasn't gambling at all but a con, and that was all right.

After she told me that, she threw back her head and laughed. That's when I saw the mole on her tongue.

Being ten, of course I asked about it. She stuck out her tongue so I could examine the growth. It was the size and shape of a navy bean. A mole on the tongue, she said, was the mark of prophetic powers. But when I begged her to tell my fortune, she wouldn't. I still remember what she said. "Some things it is better not to know."

During college I researched Romani history and culture in the library, though there wasn't a great deal to read. I knew these old women in the hospital room were keeping a death vigil. To an outsider it looked like respect, but mostly it was self-serving. If a person died with feelings of resentment or hostility toward the living, their spirit would return from the other side to haunt the offender and cause trouble. When someone was dying, old-school Romanies from far and near came to ask forgiveness for any insult or offense, in hopes of warding off a spiteful ghost.

No one spoke as I turned a slow circle in the hospice room. The sentinels watched me and I watched them. I met the eyes of all eight, one by one.

"All of you?" I said, not quietly. "All of you have wronged Gamma Rose?"

When one of them finally spoke, her voice was low-pitched and gravelly. "Who are you?"

"I'm Chantalene. Gamma Rose is my great-grandmother."

A long silence. "You're LaVita's daughter?"

"Yes."

"The daughter of a gadžo," said another.

"Yes," I said. "And you disrespected Gamma Rose because my mother married an outsider."

"They broke tradition," she said. "But Gamma Rose got even. She put a curse on my son and caused our milk cow to go dry."

"Your cow went dry because you didn't milk her," a third woman said. "And your son's just lazy. Don't speak ill of the dead."

"She isn't dead," I pointed out.

"Close enough," said the gravel-voiced one. "You have interrupted our vigil."

I turned my back, dismissing them, and leaned over the bed. Gamma's hand in mine felt weightless and dry, an origami bird. There were things about my family only she knew, knowledge that would die with her. Why hadn't I stayed in touch? Now she was dying alone among these crones, with no one who loved her.

Except me.

I leaned close to her ear, my eyes full. "Gamma Rose, it's Chantalene. LaVita's little girl. Remember me?"

The veined eyelids fluttered, and I felt the Gypsy women lean in.

"Can you wake up and talk to me? Please wake up and talk to me."

When her eyes opened, they were small and filmy. The sunken mouth worked and her tongue came out to lick dry lips. The pink mole was unmistakable.

I smiled like a quarter moon. "Gamma Rose! It's Chantalene."

She swallowed and her voice scraped. "Turn on the light. I can't see anything in here."

I pushed a button on the control attached to her bed and fluorescent light flooded the room. She squinted, then her eyes opened wider and she tried to lift her head.

"You old hags still here?" she demanded. "Get out of my room or I'll haunt you for a hundred years."

There was a flurry of blowing out candles, a rustling of long skirts. "Still mean as a badger," one of them mumbled.

"But you came to me for healing, didn't you? And to see the future," Gamma rasped.

More mumbling. "Yes, Gamma Rose. You had the gift."

"I still do. Don't forget it." Her head sank back onto the pillow.

The women began shuffling out of the room. "Rest in peace, Gamma Rose," one of them said.

"Go to hell," she said and tried to cluck her fateful tongue.

When they were gone, Gamma's eyes closed again and her breathing rasped. I didn't try to wake her. I doused the overhead light and turned on a lamp in the corner. With my chair pulled close to the bed, I began a vigil of my own.

LATER A HOSPICE worker came in to check on her. The worker's name was Jake and he was gentle and efficient. I was surprised to see a man working in hospice. Nothing in my history had led me to picture men as caregivers. This was a prejudice I now had to let go. He showed me the footrest on the chair and brought me a pillow and blanket. There was a private restroom behind a door I hadn't noticed. I hoped he was this considerate when no relative was in attendance.

I pushed back in the recliner, fidgeted, and got up to open the door a few inches. I'm more than a little claustrophobic about closed spaces. The air conditioning provided constant white noise, circulating air that smelled faintly antiseptic. I could think of worse aromas.

For a while I watched Gamma Rose sleep, her eyes twitching beneath translucent lids, dreaming the dreams of the very old. I wondered what they were. Did she remember her days as a child with the Gypsy caravan better than what happened yesterday?

She settled into a steady snore and my eyes grew heavy. I shifted to my side in the recliner and slipped into some fitful dreams of my own.

Around three a.m. Gamma Rose awoke suddenly and made a noise. I shoved aside my blanket and stood quickly. "Gamma Rose?"

Her eyes looked brighter than before, and her gaze was fixed on an empty space above the foot of her bed. Gamma Rose didn't seem to know I was there. She said something I couldn't catch, but it sounded like a question. Slowly her arms lifted, reaching out. She spoke again, strongly this time, in a language I didn't know. Perhaps it was Romani, perhaps gibberish.

Speaking to the unseen. A chill ran across my shoulders.

She smiled. I moved to the foot of the bed, hoping she would focus on me, but she continued to stare at a point above my head. She said something else. This time I was sure it was in Romani, though I couldn't understand the words. Finally her eyes closed and her arms dropped on the coverlet.

"Gamma Rose? Are you okay?"

Her face went still. I saw no rise and fall of her chest, heard no breath escape. I hammered the call button at her bedside.

Jake came immediately. I told him what happened and he placed a stethoscope on Gamma's chest and listened. I watched his eyes, holding my own breath.

"Her heart's beating," he said. "She's just sleeping soundly."

He placed each of Gamma Rose's hands under the covers and straightened her blankets. His voice was soothing. "They do this sometimes. See people who have already passed, or angels around the bed."

"Hallucinations because the brain is shutting down?"

"Maybe." Jake smiled. "Maybe not. Either way, it seems to comfort them."

Even in his scrubs he looked tanned and muscled, and I wondered what led him to this kind of work. He had an ageless face that made it hard to judge, but I guessed early forties.

After he left I paced the room, too unnerved to sleep. If only I had searched out my great-grandmother years ago, I could have learned a lot from her. Especially about the two generations of women between us. Now it might be too late. My regret weighed so heavily that I nearly missed the mumbled words that drifted from Gamma Rose's bed.

The phrase was in Romani again. "Gamma Rose? What did you say?" I leaned over her bedside and took her hand. "Can you tell me in English?"

Her eyes were closed, her breath shallow. A current passed over me, a presence of someone else in the room. Such perceptions weren't new to me, and this one was strong. Perhaps an old Gypsy spirit come to welcome Gamma Rose to the other side.

THREE

I TURNED AND shifted in the vinyl chair for what seemed like days before sunlight seeped through the blinds of the hospice room. Soft voices drifted from the hallway and footsteps passed our door. Gamma Rose was still sleeping so I left the room in search of coffee.

There had been a staff change in the night. I introduced myself to the new charge nurse, who was round and terminally cheerful. She said they would bathe Gamma Rose this morning and coax her to eat, though she'd been refusing solid food for two days. She'd been living on fruit juice and protein shakes.

"I'd like to talk to her doctor," I said. "Do you have his name?"

"Doctor Bonaparte is our gerontologist. He comes by every day after his rounds at the hospital, somewhere between ten thirty and noon."

"Thanks. I'll wait for him in her room."

She smiled, her eyes taking in my chair-hair and rumpled clothes. "Hon, that's at least four hours away. Why don't you get some breakfast while we're working with your great-grandmother? The hospital cafeteria is open, or there's a Denny's across the street. They make great pecan waffles."

The very words made my mouth water. I'd missed dinner last night. I thanked her for the tip and made my way out the sliding doors and across the two lane street, which was nearly vacant at this hour.

In a booth by the front window of the restaurant, I read a local newspaper and drank an entire pot of coffee with my waffle and scrambled eggs. I used to drink tea in the mornings, with a stick of licorice for stirring, but Drew had hooked me on coffee. The aroma conjured his image. What did it tell you when the memory of someone's face made you smile? I wondered if that face had changed since I'd seen him. My heartbeat guttered like a candle flame.

What if Drew still wanted to marry and have kids? Right now that sounded better than anything I could think of. It wouldn't be fair to tie him to a dying woman, let alone leave him with motherless babies. As I'd told Thelma, there could be an entirely different reason for his letter. That scared me even more. If he had found someone else, how would I handle that?

This line of thinking on only two hours' sleep left me shaky. Only one thing to do—I summoned the waitress and ordered dessert. Whipped cream can't cure everything, but it always helps.

I was almost finished when Jake, the hospice attendant from last night, walked past my table still wearing his scrubs. He recognized me, which was impressive since he'd seen me only in half light. He smiled and said good morning.

"Thanks for your kindness last night," I said. "I appreciate your taking good care of Gamma Rose."

His smile was sincere and showed straight white teeth. "You're welcome. How's she doing this morning?"

"Still sleeping." I hesitated to ask him about her on his time off, but did it anyway. "Any idea how much time she might have left?"

He shrugged. "There's no way of knowing. Sometimes they last longer than you think possible."

"I wish I had known sooner. But that's nobody's fault but my own."

He nodded. "Her medical records didn't list any family, and she wasn't very coherent when she came to us. I'm glad you're with her now."

He went on his way and suddenly I felt too guilty to finish my pie and whipped cream.

WHEN I RETURNED to Ozark Shepherd Hospice, an aide was in Gamma Rose's room taking her vital signs. Gamma had on a fresh gown. Her eyes were closed but I suspected she was awake because she was scowling.

"She could breathe better with oxygen," the aide said. She looked eighteen at the most and wore green scrub pants with a flowered top. "But every time we put the cannula in her nose she takes it out."

"I guess that's her choice," I said.

The girl detached the blood oxygen monitor from Gamma Rose's finger. "Umm. She had half a nutrition milkshake this morning and a little coffee." She smiled. "She does love her coffee."

As soon as the woman left, Gamma's eyes opened and fixed on me.

"Good morning," I said. "I'm Chantalene."

Her voice quavered. "I knew you were coming. It sure took you a long time."

Did she mean coming back from breakfast or coming to see her from Oklahoma? She couldn't have known that, of course, unless the Magic Mole really did have prophetic powers. I was thrilled that she seemed to know me.

"I'm sorry I took so long," I said. "But I'm here now and I'll stay."

"Get me my glasses so I can see you better."

I found them on the end table and slid the earpieces through her wild salt-and-pepper hair, which was almost as long as mine. The last time we'd met her hair was crow black. My mother had guessed she was in her early seventies then. Gamma Rose had no birth certificate. Romanies weren't good about keeping written records a century ago.

"You look like Pesha," she said. "When you first came in, I thought you were her."

I smiled. "Do you mean my mother, LaVita?"

"No. LaVita's mother, Pesha. She was beautiful."

My knees melted. I hadn't even known my grandmother's name. I pulled up a chair and leaned my arms on the bed. "Can you tell me about Pesha?"

"She rejected her husband and ran away."

"I know. And left baby LaVita with you."

She made a disapproving noise. "Pesha was a wild bird. But her voice was magic. Everybody who heard her sing fell in love with her."

"Really? I don't know anything about her. How old was she when she left?"

"Young. Seventeen, maybe."

I worried that my questions would exhaust her, but I couldn't stop, afraid this might be my only chance. "Did you ever know where she went?"

She closed her eyes. "She just disappeared." A rattling cough shook her whole body. "That bath wore me out."

"You should rest now. I'll be here when you wake up."

I sagged back in the chair, also exhausted, and turned this new fact over in my mind. I looked like my grandmother Pesha.

My mother had died young from unnatural causes, and my great-grandmother was a nonagenarian. Pesha was the tie-breaker. If Pesha had lived to a reasonable age, I could believe that I would, too.

What happened to the grandmother I never met? Maybe there were clues at Gamma Rose's house—old pictures, perhaps, or personal things Pesha had left behind. I still didn't know her married name.

Gamma Rose and I were both dozing when a man in a white jacket walked in with one of the hospice nurses.

"I'm Doctor Bonaparte," he said, and we shook hands.

"I'm Chantalene. Her great-granddaughter."

"I'm glad you're here."

He read Gamma's chart, listened to her chest, and lifted her eyelids. She kept her eyes closed, but I was pretty sure she wasn't asleep. She was quite possibly shamed at being examined by a gadžo.

The doctor lifted the covers and checked her feet and the backs of her bony legs. Finding no bedsores, he carefully covered her back up.

"She's a tough cookie," he told me.

"Yes, she is."

"Has she talked to you at all?"

"We had a short conversation this morning and she seemed to know me."

"Good." He smiled, and now that he was satisfied with Gamma's condition, he turned his interest to me. "I'm sure she's glad to see you. Where do you live?"

"Southeastern Oklahoma. I came to visit her and didn't even know she was ill."

He nodded and gestured for me to step outside with him. In the hallway, he lowered his voice. "She took a bad fall. Didn't break any bones, thankfully, but she was bruised up and badly dehydrated. It's lucky a neighbor found her and called for an ambulance.

"She has congestive heart failure and mild dementia, neither of which are surprising at her age," Dr. Bonaparte said. "Her bloodwork showed a possibility of some food poisoning, too. Sometimes these old girls use woodland plants for their own cures and do themselves more harm than good."

I nodded but said nothing.

"Anyway, those symptoms are gone," he said. "It's her heart that's the problem, and there's nothing more we can do for that. She claims to be ninety-nine. Is that right?"

"I'm not sure, but it's possible."

"Amazing." He smiled and dipped his head. "Well. It's one day at a time now. If you have any concerns, the nurses know how to reach me."

Dr. Bonaparte left to finish his rounds.

At lunchtime the aide brought a tray of soft foods. "I thought she wouldn't eat solid food," I said.

"We always offer. If she can't manage that, we'll stick with juice and the protein shake."

Gamma Rose opened her eyes and the aide adjusted the bed to a sitting position. She set the tray on a rolling table and spoke rather loudly. "You have chicken soup, applesauce, and lime gelatin. Does any of that sound good today?"

The aide handed Gamma her glasses and she eyed the plate with suspicion. She pointed a crooked finger at the soup. The aide lifted a spoonful to her lips and Gamma slurped.

"It's not hot," she said.

"No, just warm. We don't want you to burn yourself." The aide dipped another spoonful. After several of these, Gamma pointed to the applesauce. A bite of it went between the wrinkly lips and didn't come out.

The aide beamed. "You have a good appetite today!" To me she said, "She hasn't eaten this much all week." Emboldened, she offered Gamma Rose a spoonful of the gelatin.

"I don't like green Jello," Gamma said.

"Me, either," the aide said. "It must be the cook's favorite color. How about some protein shake?"

Gamma scowled again and pointed to the soup. The aide spooned up broth and a few filmy noodles. The bowl was nearly empty when Gamma Rose laid her head back and closed her eyes.

"Excellent," the young woman said. "Just one sip of water and I'll let you rest." After that she took the tray and withdrew.

Gamma looked more alert than I'd seen her yet, and she was definitely stronger.

"That canned soup is too salty," she said.

"It's good for you, though. I'm glad to see you eating."

Her eyes focused on me. "You're Chantalene."

"Yes."

"All my girls were better looking than any of those old hags' daughters." She cackled softly and I laughed, too.

I pulled my chair close. "I'd love to hear about your girls. Pesha and LaVita."

"Pesha and I grew up together," she said. "I married at sixteen and she was a little girl when my husband died."

"What did your husband die from?"

Her rheumy eyes looked into the past. "Yoors was a horse trainer, very good with them. But a snake spooked the horse and it threw him. Broke his neck."

"That must have been awful for you."

"Even worse for Pesha. She saw him die."

I opened my mouth to ask about that, but she kept talking and I did not interrupt.

"It was an arranged marriage, but I liked him. He was kind and made a good living."

Liked him, I thought. And she'd been satisfied with that. "You never remarried?"

"I never met a suitable man in the kumpania. Pesha and I were poor but happy. The trouble started when my husband's brother promised her to an older man. Pesha didn't like him. He never married but was respected because of his money. He offered a daro we couldn't refuse."

Gamma Rose wheezed and I offered some water. I felt a twinge of guilt for questioning her, but at the moment she seemed happy to talk. I couldn't miss this chance.

"What is a daro?"

Her fingers twitched, thinking on their own. "The bride price. He offered five thousand dollars. It was a fortune back then. I was very poor. We had to say yes."

I tried to understand how a mother could accept money for her daughter's marriage. It was Gypsy custom, a different world.

She closed her eyes. "Pesha never forgave me. She was in love with a frail boy in the kumpania. He was poor like us and couldn't take care of her."

"You did what you thought was best for her."

"But her husband turned out to be a brute."

"Poor Pesha," I said.

"She got pregnant right away. After the baby was born, she came to me swearing and crying. She said she hated him. That night she ran away."

"With the young man she loved?"

"Yes. This shamed her husband and he went to find her. They all disappeared."

She clamped her mouth as if to stop the quivering of her chin. Her lips turned down at the corners and disappeared in a thin arc. When she spoke again, her voice was thin.

"But I had little LaVita. She was a precious baby, not difficult like her mother."

Little LaVita. An image of my black-haired mother clouded my eyes. I wanted to know more, but Gamma Rose was talked out and closed her eyes.

———————————

AT DUSK THE old ones came again.

I helped Gamma Rose with her supper, and a nurse named Greta came to take away the tray and dispense her evening meds. Together we watched the old women file into the room and stand at the foot of Gamma's bed. Only four this time.

Their shadows hung like ghosts in the hospice room. Greta and I exchanged a glance. Neither of us quite knew what to do.

I stood. "I'm sorry, but you'll have to leave," I told the women, trying to sound polite but firm. "She doesn't want you here."

They ignored me. The one with dry ice in her voice, the tallest of the group and the boldest, wore a dark red diklo over her hair. She spoke directly to Gamma Rose in the Romani language. I once tried to learn it on my own, but with no one to model the pronunciation, my efforts were futile. All I remembered now were a few common phrases.

The old Gypsy spoke again, in English. "We apologize for all offenses and have brought Gamma Rose a gift to take with her to the other side."

She unfolded a fringed scarf and cast it like a net on the bed. Its brilliant colors—blues and purples and deep fuchsia pink—caught the last rays of light through the blinds and glistened with specks of gold. I stared at it, taken aback.

Gamma Rose spoke without opening her eyes."Te aves yertime mandar, te yertil tut o Del."

This was one phrase I knew. I forgive you and may God forgive you, too. I was witnessing a time-honored ritual.

Gamma's voice trembled. "I accept your gift. Now go away."

The tall one bowed slightly. "Peace on your journey, Gamma Rose."

"I'll tell the Devil you said hello," she said, but without rancor.

When the women had gone, Gamma Rose opened her eyes and the hint of a smile played on her face. The scarf felt like rippling water when I gathered it up and draped it across her chest.

"Definitely your color," I said.

She cackled and the Magic Mole flashed. The rich colors of the scarf reflected in her eyes.

"I've decided not to die yet," she told the nurse. "Chantalene is going to take me home."

FOUR

DESPERATE FOR SLEEP, I stayed that night at a nearby motel and met with Dr. Bonaparte the next morning at the hospital. Except for the stethoscope, he looked like a college professor—sport shirt open at the neck, his hair finger-combed, a pair of reading glasses stuck in his pocket. His direct gaze made me feel he was really listening. That specialist back in Oklahoma could have taken a lesson.

I explained Gamma Rose's sudden improvement and her desire to go home.

"Sometimes patients rally close to the end," Dr. Bonaparte said. "She might have a burst of energy or become more lucid and responsive." He raised his eyebrows. "One of my terminal patients got up and cleaned her house, then passed away peacefully that evening."

Proof positive that housecleaning kills.

The doctor shrugged. "I can't say how long she might last. If your great-grandmother wants to go home to die, she certainly has that right."

"But she can't go home alone, and she wants me to stay with her," I confessed, keeping my voice low. "Frankly, I'm terrified. Her house is isolated, and I have no experience taking care of an elderly person. Or anybody else."

I was accustomed to isolation. I'd grown up in the country and still lived there. But Gamma Rose's house sat in the deep woods, thirty miles north of nothing. I'd be alone out there with a dying woman that, truthfully, I hardly knew. For how long? I had taken five days' vacation time, expecting to be gone only four.

None of which was Dr. Bonaparte's problem. He nodded, his eyes calm. "Death is rarely convenient."

The statement made me shiver.

I am not a caregiver. Maybe it's a character flaw, but I know that about myself. Then again, the specter of my own numbered days changed a lot of things, including priorities. I was the only family Gamma Rose had, and vice versa. I knew Thelma wouldn't mind looking after my critters a few more days, and a monkey with a pencil could do my job at the local tag agency. It was a short-term position while I worked on my master's degree.

"You can still have assistance from hospice," Dr. Bonaparte assured me. "They'll come out every day, if you want. Medicare covers palliative care." He dug in his desk drawer for a card. "Here's the phone number to set it up."

It eased my mind a little to know hospice would be available to help, at least in the daytime. I knew Gamma Rose worked at a plant nursery for many years, so she should have Social Security and Medicare. Still, the prospect of watching my great-grandmother die was frightening. Had destiny sent me here to reconcile with my own death? Among those old crones in her hospice room that first night, Gamma Rose had been chillingly alone. I vowed not to desert her.

I heaved a deep breath. "Okay. So how do we transport her? An ambulance? Or can she ride in my car?"

"Let's see how strong she feels by tomorrow," he said. "The nurse had her up in the geri chair for breakfast this morning, and she did fine."

"What's a geri chair?"

"Short for geriatric. It's a wheelchair with extra features and padding especially for elderly patients. You can take the chair with you. Hospice will provide a walker, too, but don't let her walk around unless you're holding onto her. The last thing she needs is another fall."

He said the charge nurse at Ozark Shepherd would go over "details of her care" with me, a prospect that made me cringe.

When I was a teenager, my foster mother said that in her day, a girl growing up on an Oklahoma farm had four choices. She could become a farm wife, a teacher, a secretary, or a nurse. I told her if those were my options, I'd shoot myself. Now, I was about to take on the role of nurse, and no one could be less suited for the job.

I tried to talk Gamma Rose out of going home by being honest about my limitations. "I don't know how to take care of you the way they do here."

She dismissed my concerns. "We'll be fine. We're family." She patted my hand.

I could tell from her tone that there was no changing her mind. I began filling out paperwork.

The next day, with my heartbeat drilling like a manic woodpecker, I loaded Gamma Rose into my Honda with the help of Nurse Greta. She was plumb and efficient, with freckled cheeks and a cheerful smile. She volunteered to follow me in her own car and help us get settled. Greta was my new best friend.

The geri chair was folded up in the back, and bags of groceries I'd bought that morning clumped together on the rear seat. I had no idea what I'd find when we arrived at Gamma's little house in the woods.

Greta's tan car fell behind as we drove the two-lane highway from Madison toward Crooked Dog Creek. I have a tendency to speed. When I lost sight of her in the rearview mirror, I took my foot off the gas and glanced over at Gamma Rose. She was barely tall enough to see over the dashboard and looked more frail in the car than she had in bed.

"How are you doing?" I asked.

"I'm a new woman."

We both laughed. I was coming to enjoy her scratchy voice.

I didn't inherit Gamma Rose's magic mole, thank goodness, but I do sometimes have premonitions, and I see auras. This usually happens when I'm calm and centered, or occasionally when I'm suppressing strong emotion. Thelma and Drew were the only humans who knew about this ability. My dog knew of course. Dogs know everything. I never mentioned it to my rural neighbors, who already considered me an outsider, and therefore suspicious, even though I grew up there. The fact that I perversely enjoyed outsider status only confirmed their judgment.

Gamma Rose's aura was faded and very shallow. It made me sad for both of us. She watched the autumn scenery slide past the windows with no expression. She was wearing a nightgown with the new silk scarf draped around her shoulders. Its vivid colors jaundiced her sallow skin. Her hair lay in black-and-silver tufts against the seatback. I wished for the talent to capture her venerable face on canvas. Failing that, I promised myself I'd take her picture in that scarf, if she'd let me.

It took twenty minutes to reach the post office at Crooked Dog Creek and twenty more to wind through the mountains to Gamma Rose's home. I would have missed the driveway, hidden by trees and kudzu vines, if she hadn't pointed it out. I paused at the entrance to be sure Greta saw where we turned.

The driveway had once been graveled but was now mostly dirt. It was long, rough, and wreathed in branches. At the end sat a wooden cabin that looked as if it might have grown up from the earth. The house seemed much smaller than it had when I was ten. Faded green shingles, covered with moss and leaves, sheltered the peaked roof. An electric line sagged from a utility pole toward the eaves, and a ladder-like antenna lay prone on the roof.

Calico curtains showed through the windows, but my heart froze when I saw an old-fashioned water pump in the yard and a WPA-era outhouse half hidden in the trees. My god, did the house not have modern plumbing? I tried to remember that detail from my childhood visit here but could not.

Greta parked beside us in the yard. Sunlight glinted from the rump of an old car parked under the trees. Grass and weeds had grown up around it. If Gamma Rose didn't drive anymore, how did she get her groceries and other needs? I saw no fence around the house and no animals roaming, but a small chicken coop sat to one side of the yard, its wire gate open.

My nose wrinkled. "You keep chickens?"

The reason I hate chickens is a grisly story from my childhood. Let's just say if I believed in minions of the devil, I'd assign the role to those brainless beasts. Give me snakes, scorpions, tarantulas—I'd take them all, and sic 'em on the chickens.

"They let my hens loose when they took me away," Gamma said. "The girls will come home when we throw out some feed."

Swell.

I popped the tailgate and set up the geri chair. There was a single step at the front door, which looked too narrow for the wheelchair.

"We'll have to carry her from there," Greta said.

Greta parked the chair by the passenger-side door and smoothly transferred my great-grandmother aboard. The chair's wheels rattled over the ground, but Gamma Rose didn't complain. Greta pushed open the front door—which wasn't locked, I noted—and we made a Girl Scout saddle with our arms. Greta coaxed Gamma Rose to put her arms around our necks and trust our strength. She weighed no more than a child and we carried her easily, maneuvering sideways through the door.

The darkness inside was blinding. We waited a moment, our eyes adjusting. The air smelled dusty and stale.

"On the sofa," Gamma said, but there was so much furniture in the room that our four-legged carriage couldn't shuffle through.

"Maybe the bedroom," Greta suggested.

We lowered her onto the unmade bed and removed her scarf and slippers. She looked exhausted but said she didn't want to sleep. She asked me to prop her up, and I did my best with the two pillows.

"Somebody's been here," she groused. "I never leave my bed unmade."

"Maybe you just got up when you fell," Greta said. "The neighbor found you still in your nightgown."

"I don't remember that."

She closed her eyes, which I'd come to recognize as a coping device when she was confused or unhappy. I drew a patchwork quilt over her legs and spread the scarf on the foot of the bed. Her breath was sawing before Greta and I slipped out the door.

I stood a moment in the living room, surveying the chaos. In a space no bigger than a rich woman's closet, there was a sofa, two easy chairs, a coffee table, two end tables with lamps, a bookshelf, and two straight chairs. There was no TV, despite the antenna on the roof. Knickknacks covered all flat surfaces.

"Wow," I said.

Greta gave a small laugh. "Shall we air out the place?"

With considerable effort, we got one of the two front windows open. Fresh air drafted between it and the door. It was a beautiful October day in the Ozarks.

"That must be the kitchen," I said, and wandered through an arched doorway, dreading what I'd find.

But the kitchen was neat as an OCD's sock drawer. No dirty dishes in the sink, a clean rug on the linoleum floor. It was cluttered, mostly with decorative chickens, but everything was in its place. A current calendar hung on the wall by the phone.

There was even a phone and running water!

Feeling optimistic, I went to check out the bathroom. It had almost-modern conveniences. With a flush toilet and a claw-footed bathtub, I had no complaints.

But how did Gamma Rose get in and out of that tub? There was no shower. I suspected she'd been getting by with bird baths for quite some time.

There was only one bedroom. I'd have to use that hammock of a sofa for my bed, but I don't sleep much anyway.

"Let's see what's in the refrigerator," Greta said.

She opened the fridge door and peered inside. "Unh." Two dishes covered in plastic wrap were filled with grayish green fuzz. She shrugged. "She's been gone two weeks, after all."

I liked her for defending my great granny's housekeeping. But I suspected we might have found the source of Gamma's food-poisoning symptoms.

Together we cleaned out the fridge and dusted the tchotchkes in the living room, occasionally peeking in to find Gamma Rose still napping. I put away the groceries and Greta unloaded supplies from her car. She'd brought an aluminum frame that fitted around the toilet to make it easier for Gamma Rose to get up, and several boxes of adult diapers "in case you can't get her to the bathroom in time." Greta leaned a folded walker beside the front door and unpacked a kit containing geri-wipes, lip balm, gauze bandages with paper tape, Dulcolox, antibiotic salve, and skin lotion. I was thoroughly intimidated.

"Watch out for bedsores," she said. "Their old skin is so tender. If she can't get out of bed, you'll need to turn her at least twice a day."

Panic set it. "When will you be back?"

"Every afternoon, if you want. It won't be me every time, but someone on our staff. All our people are trained to do the bathing and attend to minor medical needs."

"I'm really out of my comfort zone here."

She gave me an encouraging smile. "Believe me, you're not the first caregiver to feel anxious. I'm really glad she has family with her."

When everything was squared away, I walked with her to the dooryard. It was with sincere regret that I watched Greta's car bump down the long driveway. It disappeared into thick foliage that soon obscured the engine's sound.

Quiet closed in around me. I stood on the front step listening to the breathing of trees. There was almost no wind, which seemed freakish to a native Oklahoman.

Then I recognized the whit-whit-whit-cheer! of a cardinal. A squirrel chattered from the oaks and flipped his tail like a whip. I looked up and smiled at him. Gold leaves spiraled down, and I detected a soft sound like rushing water from the hills behind the house. The place was truly beautiful. I imagined hiking through the trees to find an Ozark stream.

The woods were lovely, dark and deep, and I made a promise I intended to keep. I can do this, Gamma Rose. Whatever you need.

I was sincerely glad I had come. I still hoped to find my matriarchal history, and this house was the source of those waters. My mother had grown up in these woods. My grandmother Pesha, who married a man she didn't love and ran off with a man she did, disappeared from here without a trace. I went inside to check on my great-grandmother and start my search.

WHILE GAMMA ROSE slept that afternoon, I dug through shelves and drawers. Romanies weren't big on written records. I knew I wouldn't find a Bible with the family tree inscribed in fading ink. I found no papers at all, just a box of faded photographs, most of them black and white. Old photos always fascinated me. I turned on both lamps and set the box on the coffee table with great anticipation.

The lamps were barely better than candles, and the mahogany paneling sucked up what light they gave. I pushed back the window curtains as far as they would go and squinted at pictures of dark-haired, dark-eyed strangers. Most of the adults were posed and unsmiling. A few candid shots showed small children being bathed in wash tubs or clinging to their mother's skirts. None of the pictures had identification, no writing on the back with names or years. These were Romani people and could be my relatives, but I had no way of knowing.

In several pictures, men in their fanciest attire stood beside shining vehicles, obviously proud of their rides. The vintage autos were my only clue to the dates of the photos. I'd never paid much attention to cars. If it had four wheels and ran, it was okay with me. Luckily, I recognized old models better than new ones. I identified finned Chevies and Caddies from the late 1950s and early 1960s. By my calculations, Pesha would have disappeared somewhere in the '60s. I put those photos aside and shuffled through the stack again, looking for the same men in pictures that included women. It was an unscientific method, and the photos were regrettably fuzzy.

Despite the open window, the house felt stuffy and I was sweating. I spied a dusty box fan wedged in a corner behind the lamp table and turned it on. With no air conditioning, what must the house feel like in steamy July or August, when temperatures here could hit the nineties?

I put away the box and laid my selected pictures on the bookshelf. When Gamma was having a bright moment, maybe she could identify the people. I dared not wait long to ask.

But right now, I needed to fix something for an early dinner. Neither of us had eaten lunch.

Not organized enough to do any real cooking, I settled on beef and vegetable soup with some soft, sour-dough bread and butter. I trimmed the crusts from Gamma's bread. She needed calories that were easy to chew. The soup was canned, the low sodium kind because she'd complained about canned soup at the hospice facility being too salty. I lit the gas burner with a match, its explosive flame nearly taking off my eyebrows, and set the soup to heating. Then I went to rouse Gamma Rose if I could.

She was already awake. "You're still here," she said, and smiled at me with surprisingly good teeth. The pleasure in her eyes made me glad we'd brought her home.

I smiled back. "Still here. Are you hungry?"

"A little. I'll come to the kitchen."

Whoa. I had thought to feed her in bed. But the doctor said moving around would increase her circulation and reduce the chance of bed sores. I pushed the geri chair next to the bed. "Okay, here we go. Swing your legs out first."

She eyed the chair. "I'll just walk."

"Not a good idea, Gamma Rose. If you fall, we're both in trouble. For today let's use the chair." I looked at her stern face. "Please?"

"Huh," she said, which I took for grudging assent.

We got her upright, turned her butt toward the chair, and lowered her in. "Do you need to go to the bathroom?" I dreaded the answer something fierce.

"Not now," she said.

"Good then. Let's eat."

Luckily the chair fit through the bedroom door, but I had to move a flowered chair in the living room in order to navigate a path to the kitchen. I heard the soup bubbling as I rolled her up to the table.

I opened a cabinet door. "Which soup bowls should I use?"

"That blue one's mine," she said. "You can use yellow. Visitors' utensils are in that drawer over there."

"All righty." I dished hers up to cool and fixed her a glass of water and a slice of bread with butter. "If you can't chew the beef in this soup, just leave it alone, or I'll pick it out for you. I don't eat red meat, so I'm taking it out of mine." I hoped what remained would give us both some protein.

I set our bowls on the table. "We'd better let it cool a minute." She nodded, and we sat with our hands in our laps.

"Why don't you eat meat?" she said.

"I don't know. At some point it just turned me off."

"LaVita didn't like meat either. Or maybe that was Pesha. I forget."

"Maybe it's inherited then. I've been looking through your old photos this afternoon. I hope you don't mind."

"What photos?"

"In that box in your bookshelf."

"I don't remember those."

I tested the soup. It was just right. "Can you feed yourself, or shall I help?"

"I can do it." Her hand trembled so much that she had to lean close over the bowl. I watched, using body English to help her. When half a spoonful went in successfully, she smacked. "Needs salt."

I tried not to laugh. I sprinkled a little salt into her bowl and stirred it.

"That's better," she said, even before she tasted it again.

There wasn't much conversation after that. She managed the pieces of mushy beef just fine and hummed after every bite. When we were finished I washed our dishes—separately, by Romani custom—and steered her chair to the bathroom.

Getting her situated was like wrestling a bag full of water, but once seated she took care of the rest. I helped her back into the chair and we rolled toward the living room.

"I always sit outdoors after supper," she said.

I hedged, thinking of how Greta and I carried her up the front step. "There's no place to sit out there," I said. "And we can't get your chair out the door."

"Those straight chairs go outside." She pointed. "I just bring them in when it rains."

That explained the eroded varnish. "How do you spend your evenings when it rains, or in the winter?" I asked, hoping to distract her.

"I used to have a TV, but it quit."

"And after that?" I wasn't sure she'd ever learned to read. There wasn't a book in the house except the two I'd brought. The bookshelf was occupied by tchotchkes.

"I used to make lace, before my hands got crippled up."

"Really! What a wonderful skill. Did you make these doilies on the sofa?"

"Those aren't lace," she said disdainfully. "Those are crocheted. I bought 'em at the Walmart in Madison."

"Oh. So after you gave up making lace, how do you pass the time now?"

She thought it over, her mouth working inside her sunken cheeks. "I just sit there and listen."

I was torn between the loneliness of that image and a sense of awe. Maybe old folks knew more about meditation than those of us who practiced it daily using learned instructions. Just sit and listen.

"Carry those two chairs out," she ordered. "Then help me get outside."

The idea of sitting in the cool outdoors instead of the airless house made me bold. "Okay. Don't try to get up by yourself." I carried the two chairs outside.

We must have looked like a female Laurel and Hardy. I rolled the geri chair close to the door, set the walker in front of it, and helped her stand up. She hadn't used a walker before she went to the hospital and it was still new to her. The leg caught on the door jamb. The thing tipped and she launched a few cuss words with which I fully agreed. I shoved the apparatus aside.

"Okay, the walker probably isn't a good idea for getting down the step, anyway," I said. She was so light I might have been able to carry her, but what if I stumbled? Instead, I put my arm around her waist, which wasn't easy because she was about five-one and I'm five-seven. "Now put your arm around my waist and hang onto my other hand like we're dancing," I said. "That's it. Good. When I say ready, we'll step down together. Ready!"

I hoped the tail of her nightgown didn't catch on her foot. But of course it did. She tripped and I caught her. When she was righted, we took baby steps toward the closest chair. We must have looked like a unisex version of Astaire and Gaynor. I couldn't keep from smiling.

We eased her onto the wooden seat. Neither chair had arms and it suddenly occurred to me she might fall off. Should I tie her in?

"Stop fussing," she groused. "I could have done that step easier by myself."

I pulled my chair within arm's reach of hers. Finally settled, we both huffed and gazed into the mute woods.

The sun disappeared behind the hills, and stately trees stood close around us. Dusk would come early here. A wayward breeze crossed my skin like cool water.

The woods went dark from the inside out. Nightfall collected deep in the trees and unfurled toward our feet. An owl hooted. The creatures of the night were afoot.

I was almost relaxed when Gamma Rose's arms slowly lifted. She reached toward something hidden from me, her eyes focused far away. Seeing the unseen. Her face was calm.

"What is it, Gamma Rose?" I said quietly. "What do you see?"

"Somebody drove up," she said. "I think it's Pesha. And a man."

There was no car anywhere near us. "Who is the man, can you tell?"

Long pause. "Don't know him," she said. "But he's a stubby little son of a bitch."

She said something in Romani, then her hands dropped to her lap. I put my arm around her shoulders to steady her. Her chin dropped to her chest and I thought she'd gone to sleep—or died.

"Gamma Rose? Gamma Rose!"

Her eyes opened and she smiled at me. "You're still here."

"Still here."

"I'm glad you came, Pesha."

The night sifted down and settled on our shoulders. We sat and listened.

FIVE

MY FIRST NIGHT in Gamma Rose's house, I didn't sleep much. Through the open window I heard the rustle of animal footsteps in fallen leaves. A pair of owls called to each other in the distance. Gamma Rose roused once in the night, talking to herself or to the unseen, but she soon dozed off again. We both awoke with the sun.

At breakfast, Gamma ate a few bites of oatmeal and sat in her geri chair keeping me company while I worked in the kitchen. She'd begun to take ownership of the padded chair. It supported her so she could cat nap without tipping sideways. Her gnarled hands rested on the fold-up tray.

At mid-morning, I heard a vehicle coming up the driveway. I was deboning a chicken for soup, a task that gave me malicious satisfaction. It wasn't one of Gamma Rose's hens, though I wasn't above offing a Leghorn if one of them returned from exile. She had instructed me—at daybreak—to put out chicken feed and water. As I'd filled the pan and scattered pellets across the yard, I wondered what else we might be luring in from the woods.

Apparently there was nothing feeble about Gamma's hearing. She heard the engine noise almost as soon as I did and lifted her chin. "Somebody's coming."

"Maybe it's Greta, from the hospice service," I said.

She frowned. "No. It's somebody else."

Could she tell by the sound of the car? Or was this the Magic Mole's prediction?

I washed my hands and rolled Gamma to the front door. Sure enough, the vehicle pulling into the yard was not Greta's tan compact but a dark blue pickup. The man who got out was slender and wore jeans and a tee-shirt. He carried a zippered bag in one hand and a paper sack in the other. I ruled out a local farmer or rancher because he wasn't wearing a hat.

A sudden awareness of vulnerability elbowed me. Back home I lived in a farmhouse on sixty acres, and I was comfortable being alone. But I had a loaded shotgun within quick reach and a tall dog who was suspicious of strangers. Gamma Rose had no such protections, and I realized how easily we might fall prey to someone with bad intentions.

Luckily, this visitor turned out to be a friend, hailing us with a wave as he approached. "Good morning! I'm Jake from Ozark Shepherd Hospice."

I hadn't recognized him out of his scrubs. He was prettier than Greta, but she was my safety net and I was disappointed. "Greta couldn't come?"

"She had another client this morning and didn't want to make you wait all day."

I tried not to look like a lost puppy. Surely Greta would come tomorrow.

He focused on Gamma Rose and smiled. "Hello, Miss Rose. You're looking well today."

"So are you," she said and he laughed.

"I met you at the Ozark Shepherd facility," he told her. "Do you remember?"

She shook her head. "No. I know you from someplace else. I think we're related."

He grinned. "Well, you probably know a lot of people."

"Too many," she said.

Jake glanced at me and winked. He raised the paper sack he'd brought. "Greta sent you some things. May I come in?"

"Of course," I said and moved Gamma Rose back from the doorway.

Jake paused inside, blinking, just as I had done yesterday. Then he set his things on the coffee table. If he was taken aback by the abundance of furniture, his face didn't show it.

He smiled at Gamma and took a stethoscope and blood pressure cuff from the zipper bag. "I'm glad to see you up and around. Let's check your vital signs this morning."

"Why?" she said.

He squatted beside her chair—sideways, for lack of space—and looked at her earnestly. "That's a fair question. It's one of the things I'm supposed to do so we'll know if you're hurting or need the doctor to visit. But if you don't want to, I'll just write down that you told me to buzz off."

He had a great smile, and I saw Gamma's resistance melt.

"All right," she said. "But don't pump that thing so tight. It hurts my arm."

"Noted," he said, and snapped on latex gloves. "I hate these things, but they're required. To protect the patient and me both, they say."

"Makes sense," I put in. "How long have you worked with Ozark Shepherd?"

"About three months. I was an EMT up in Missouri until the company downsized." He placed the business end of the scope to Gamma Rose's chest and listened.

Probably there weren't many job opportunities for a laid-off EMT in a town as small as Madison. I wondered why he came to Madison, but it was none of my business. Maybe he had roots around here. The pull of the past could be strong, if not always pleasant. I was the poster girl for that.

Jake took Gamma's blood pressure as carefully as he could, noted the results on his chart, and registered her temperature with a swipe of a thermometer across her forehead. "Your blood pressure is better than mine," he teased. "Want to go dancing tonight?"

"Maybe tomorrow," she said. He had won the old girl over.

He put away his things. "Would you like a bath this morning?"

That put a different look on her face.

"No!"

"I'm guessing you'd rather have Greta do that," Jake said and turned to me. "That's okay. With her dry skin, twice a week is often enough unless she has an accident."

"Her bathroom has a claw-footed tub. I was worried about the bath."

"Greta can give her a bed bath. Much safer." He took off the gloves and put them in his pocket. From the paper sack, he produced an amber pill vial that he handed to me. "Doctor Bonaparte sent these. They help guard against fluid accumulating around her heart. Directions are on the label."

He reached in the sack again and came out with a junior-sized Bundt cake wrapped in plastic. "Now for the good stuff!"

Gamma Rose's eyes followed the cake to its resting place on the table.

"We noticed you liked the rum cake when you stayed with us," Jake said. "So we asked the cook to make you one."

"That cake is good," Gamma said.

Jake winked at her. "They tell me the secret is Mexican dark rum."

"I'll put it in the kitchen," I said. "We can have some for lunch."

"Let's have some now," she said.

I smiled, pleased that her appetite had returned. "Why not?"

I served her cake on a paper plate on the geri chair's tray. Jake declined and I satisfied myself with a pinch of crumbs. Delicious.

Jake was in no hurry to get back. Maybe spending time with the client was part of the job. While Gamma Rose hummed over her cake, he sat on the sofa and made conversation, asking where I came from and about my family connection with the local Romani. The questions might have seemed intrusive from someone else, but his expression was so open that I couldn't be offended. He was one of those people who are genuinely interested in the details of other people's lives.

When I mentioned leaving my farm, horse, and dog in the care of a friend, he asked about Bones.

"She's a black and white border collie mix," I said and showed him a picture on my phone. He reciprocated immediately, scrolling to a photo of a large, hairy mutt.

"This is T-Bone. He's a mix, too, but mostly lab. He runs with me, hikes with me. Even sleeps on my bed." Jake grinned like a proud father, swiping through one photo after another.

I had the feeling he'd asked about my dog as a pretext for showing off pictures of his own. I'm a dog person too, so I was fine with that. T-Bone was chocolate brown with a fuzzy muzzle that hinted at his mixed heritage.

When Jake finally ran out of photos, I indulged my own curiosity and asked how he came to be an EMT.

"By accident," he said. "I started med school in Missouri but ran out of money and had to quit and go to work. I liked the EMT training, the emergency aspect of saving lives. So I stuck with that until the city cut back services."

"Will you go back to med school at some point?"

He shrugged. "I'd have to start over, if they'd even let me in. Besides, it's hard to save much on a hospice worker's salary. I'm not brave enough to borrow huge sums of money."

"There are worse things than debt," I said quietly. "Like running out of time."

He flashed the smile again. "I guess if I ran out of time before I paid off my student loans, the government couldn't sue me."

Gamma Rose's eyes had closed and her head drooped at an angle that hurt my neck. "Looks like she's ready for a nap," Jake said. "Shall we get her to bed?"

At bedside he lifted her from the chair so gently she didn't wake up. I made the bed that morning on her orders so he laid her on the spread. I noticed his sculpted arms and nicely rounded backside as he bent to lay Gamma on the bed. Jake kept himself in shape. I covered Gamma's legs with an extra quilt.

"How did you get along last night?" Jake asked.

"Pretty well," I said. "She woke up once and said her mouth was dry. I gave her a sip of water and put some of that salve on her lips. Then she slept until six."

"She should have an oxygen unit. It would help her breathe better. I'll have Greta bring one when she comes tomorrow." He followed me into the living room. "What about you? Did you get any sleep?"

"Not much," I admitted. "But I think I've memorized all the sounds of the house and the woods. Tonight I'll probably sleep like a rock."

He retrieved his nursing kit and saw my crime novel on the table. "I've read that." His eyebrows raised. "It's good, but it might give you the creeps at night, out here so far from civilization."

"Civilization is what gives me the creeps," I said. "I don't mind solitude."

"That's lucky. You'll have plenty of it."

I walked outdoors with him. "I keep thinking I hear a stream somewhere behind the house."

"You do." He pointed. "It comes down from that mountain and eventually runs into Crooked Dog Creek."

"You know this area?"

"I'm sort of an ecology nerd. I volunteer with a conservation group that works to protect the Ozarks. I also do a lot of hiking."

"Good therapy, I imagine, after working every day with people who are dying."

He gave me an amused look. "My hospice work isn't depressing."

"Really. I can see you're much closer to enlightenment than I am."

"I don't know about that. But I learn a great deal about life, and dignity, from our patients. You may be surprised at what you learn from Miss Rose."

I did hope to learn from her, but not about the process of dying.

He tossed his bag in the truck and got in. "Anything Greta or I can bring you next time, besides the oxygen machine?"

I thought about that. I'd brought my laptop, but there was no internet service out here so it wasn't much good for entertainment. "Not unless I run out of books and need to borrow one."

"I'll give you my cell number." He wrote on the back of a generic Ozark Shepherd Hospice card and handed it out the window. "Unless you have the local wireless service, reception out here is terrible. But you can reach me from Miss Rose's land line."

"Thanks."

"Call anytime. If I'm with a patient I'll call back as soon as I can." His smile changed slightly as I met his dark eyes. "Maybe we can go for a hike some time. Find that stream."

"That sounds like fun."

He started the engine and I watched his truck rumble down the driveway until it disappeared into the trees.

Greta who?

INSIDE, THE HOUSE was quiet and the day yawned. I came face to face with the enemy of the full-time caretaker—boredom.

Suddenly I was homesick. Did Bones miss me? Was Whippoorwill wondering why we hadn't gone riding? I pulled out my cell phone to call Thelma, but Jake was right. My cell had no service. I'd have to use Gamma Rose's red kitchen phone.

Thelma answered on the third ring and assured me everything back home was fine. "I brought Bones to my house yesterday to play with Sparky, but at dusk she lit out for home."

I was proud of her faithfulness. A dog on the porch makes a house look occupied.

"I'm going to be here longer than I thought," I said. "Gamma Rose was in a hospice facility when I got here, but she wanted me to bring her home. Nobody knows how long she might last."

"I'm sorry to hear that. Do whatever you need to, and I'll look after the farm. But keep me posted. I couldn't get through on your cell."

"Yeah, that's a problem. Let me give you Gamma Rose's land line number."

Thelma wrote it down. "Learn anything yet about your missing grandma? And did you answer Drew's letter?"

"Yes and no," I said. "I don't know what to say to him."

"Tell him it's okay to come see you. No sense trying to guess what's on his mind."

"You're right. I should call him."

I told her what little I'd learned about Pesha then said good-bye. I wasn't ready to talk to Drew. Not yet. I wanted more information about my maternal history.

I shuffled through the stack of old photos again and decided to ask Gamma Rose about them today. With nothing else to do, I took my crime novel outdoors to read in the sunshine, leaving the front door open so I could hear her if she called.

The air was warm and lazy. A crow cawed in the distance and thunder clouds were building behind the hills to the west. I sighed and settled down in my chair.

Jake was right about the book, too. It got creepier and creepier. I loved it and had just finished chapter ten when I detected movement in my peripheral vision. A young woman was coming up the driveway on foot. She was dressed in jeans, a close-fitting top, and pink flip-flops. She had seen me before I saw her and raised a hand in greeting.

At closer range, I realized she was a teenager. Dark hair and eyes, olive skin, and features that were striking if not pretty. A Romani. The defiance in her body language was transparent. I could tell she was uneasy about approaching a stranger.

I smiled and tried to look nonthreatening. "Hello. Have you come to see Gamma Rose? I'm her great-granddaughter."

"I heard you were here." She didn't smile back. "I came to ask Gamma Rose for a reading."

"A reading?"

"Does she use cards or palms?"

The light dawned. I closed my book. "I don't know. I didn't even know she gave readings."

"I don't think she has for a long time. My grandmother said she has the gift and that I'd better come quick before she passed."

Wasn't this interesting. I wondered if her grandma was one of those who had come to the hospice in Madison.

"How far have you walked?" I said.

"Not far. My sister is waiting in the car at the road."

"Ah. I'm sorry to disappoint you, but Gamma is sleeping. She does that a lot now."

The girl nodded. "I'll wait."

She stood there watching me, and I sat there watching her. This went on for a full minute, until thunder grumbled and a gust of wind swept the yard. "Would you like something cold to drink?"

"Thank you," she said, and followed me toward the house as quarter-sized raindrops splattered the ground.

I offered her iced tea, which she accepted since I didn't have Cokes. "I'm Chantalene," I said. "What's your name?"

"Lucinda."

"You want Gamma Rose to tell your future?"

"Just my love life. I know she won't do the rest, like, how long I'll live or how I'll die."

I smiled, remembering my same request at age ten. "Yeah, she wouldn't do that for me, either."

A scratchy voice emanated from the bedroom. "Who's out there?"

Lucinda looked at me, a flash of apprehension in her eyes. With no manners at all, I hollered back. "It's Lucinda. She's come for a reading about her love life."

I kept my face admirably neutral. Lucinda and I watched each other for several silent moments.

"Mimi's granddaughter?" Gamma Rose called.

Lucinda nodded. "Yes," I answered. "I'll bring her in."

We heard mumbling, which I ignored. "Come on." I couldn't wait to see this.

The girl followed me through the living room furniture gallery to Gamma's bedroom. She was waiting with a practiced scowl on her face.

"Gamma Rose, this is Lucinda," I said and urged the girl forward.

"I don't give readings anymore," Gamma said.

Lucinda knelt beside the bed. "Please, Miz Gamma Rose. My boyfriend wants to get married. He says he loves me, but I don't know if I can trust him. He's too handsome. Girls are always after him."

Gamma's mouth worked, her small eyes shifting around the ceiling. Lightning flashed and the lamplight wavered. Rain tattooed the shingles. "Who is this boyfriend?"

"His name is Rondo."

A crack of thunder jolted Lucinda and me but didn't faze Gamma Rose. "That's not his name," she said. "That's what he calls himself to sound tough."

The girl's eyes widened. "His name is Ronald Lavollo."

"Son of Jason and Dritta?"

"Yes."

"How old is he?"

"He's nineteen. He finished high school," she added.

Gamma licked her lips, flashing the pink mole on her tongue. "Give me your hand."

Lucinda offered her hand, palm up. Gamma's claw-like fingers looked ancient against the girl's smooth skin. She glanced at the palm, licked her lips again, and closed her eyes. "He's been slipping around to another woman's house while you're in school. Someone older, more experienced. If you marry him now, you'll regret it."

Lucinda burst into tears. "That's what my grandma said, but I didn't believe her."

"Don't ask for the truth if you don't want to know."

"I did want to know," the girl said, sniffing and straightening her face. "I suspected him but couldn't be sure. Thank you, Gamma Rose."

She backed out of the room and I heard quick footsteps leaving the house. I gave Gamma Rose a skeptical look.

"The Lavollo men are all worthless," she said. "Doesn't take a special gift to know that."

I grinned.

"But this Ronald," she said, quite serious, "he will die young."

The smile melted from my face. "How do you know?"

"I saw him when he was born," she said. "Help me to the bathroom now."

ENCOURAGED BY GAMMA Rose's alertness with Lucinda, in late afternoon I moved some furniture in the living room and fitted her geri chair beside the coffee table. This was easier now that the two straight chairs were outdoors. I brought out the stack of old photographs.

"Can you tell me who these people are?"

At the sight of faces from long ago, her eyes went flat and her lips tightened. I held up one picture after another.

She shook her head. "I don't remember."

I kept trying. The only face she identified was a man she called Uncle Luca, her husband's brother who had arranged Pesha's marriage. This was the uncle's duty, she explained, when a girl's father died. Luca was dead now, too.

After half a dozen photos, she took off her glasses and closed her eyes. Her breath sounded labored. It occurred to me belatedly how sad it would be to outlive your friends and family. The only people who shared memories from her marriage or childhood had been gone for years. I understood her loneliness in a way I hadn't before.

I put away the pictures and made us some lunch.

To pass the time that afternoon, I read aloud to her from my crime novel, the only reading material in the house. I skipped the parts that might be too graphic, but I don't think it would have mattered. She was listening, but not to me.

As the sun touched the top of the mountains, the room gradually filled with shadows. I stopped reading when I noticed Gamma Rose frowning.

She lifted her hand and paused a long time. I thought she was going to speak to someone unseen again, but instead she said, "Where does that door go?"

"Which door?"

She stared toward the thickening darkness in a corner beside the bookshelf. "It wasn't there before," she said.

"That's just a shadow, Gamma Rose," I said gently. "It isn't a door."

Her face was blank. I couldn't tell if she'd understood me.

"That must be where he comes in," she said.

My heart felt sick. I went to the corner and put my hand against the paneling. "There's no door here. See? Just a shadow on the walls." She continued to stare, seeing something I couldn't.

When the kitchen phone rang, I jumped like a rabbit. Gamma Rose looked puzzled by the sound. I guessed her phone didn't ring very often. There was no one left who would call. I hurried toward the kitchen.

"Hi, it's Greta from Ozark Shepherd Hospice," the caller said. "If it's okay, I'll come out around ten tomorrow morning. I'll bring an oxygen machine and do Missus Tsura's bath."

I told her what had just happened with Gamma Rose.

"Sundowners," she said.

"I beg your pardon?"

"When the light changes, old folks sometimes see things in the shadows. The room looks different to them. It's called sundowners syndrome because it often happens at dusk."

A shiver ran up my back. I was learning things I wished I didn't know.

THE EVENING WAS too wet for us to sit outdoors. I was still hoping to talk about Pesha, but Gamma Rose felt dizzy after dinner and by eight-thirty she was ready for bed. I helped her beneath the covers and remembered the pills Jake had brought. The directions said one before bedtime. Gamma swallowed the tablet with some difficulty and fell into a heavy sleep. I wondered if the "burst of energy" Dr. Bonaparte had spoken of had run its course.

Her withered face lay slack and pallid against the pillow. She was slipping away and there was nothing I could do. Melancholy hunched black and feathered on my shoulders as I left her room.

I did not believe Gamma Rose's mind was so damaged by dementia that she couldn't recognize her own daughter in those photos. She remembered a lot of things when she wanted to. Why wouldn't she tell me which one was Pesha? I suspected she knew what happened to my grandmother, and maybe whether she was alive or dead.

I thought of her prediction for Ronald Lavollo. Could Gamma Rose foresee that I would die young?

Don't ask for the truth if you don't want to know.

SIX

WITH GAMMA ROSE tucked in for the night, I stood in the open front door and wondered what to do for the rest of the evening. It was much too early for me to sleep. The rain-cooled air felt like satin on my skin, and the scent of wet bark and decaying leaves drifted from the woods. Maybe Jake didn't find his hospice work depressing, but I had to get out of that stuffy house or start howling at the moon.

I decided on a short jog.

Gamma's flashlight cast a watery yellow oval on the kitchen floor. I pounded it against the heel of my hand until the beam brightened. If I stayed on the driveway, I could find my way back to the house in case the light went out. I laced up my sneakers, grabbed my hoodie, and set out at jail-break pace across the damp yard.

An archway of trees blotted out the sky and clouds obscured the moon. The woods were unbelievably dark and the night sounds were different from the day. Leaves dripped. Something scurried into the underbrush. The baritone hoot of a great horned owl, very close, vibrated in my sternum. Far away, its mate answered, an alto.

In Oklahoma, most roads are laid out in north-south or east-west grids. Here, no road ran straight and the sky was narrow. By the time I'd followed the curving driveway to the blacktop road, I had directional vertigo. If it weren't for the gravel path, I wouldn't have had a clue how to get back to Gamma Rose's cabin.

I stood at the mouth of the driveway and tried to reckon whether the route we'd driven coming in, past Crooked Dog Creek post office, was left or right from here. If I could pin that down, maybe the hills would stop revolving. I remembered turning right off the blacktop into her driveway, and that meant we'd arrived on the road that was now to my left. I peered hard into the darkness and recognized nothing. Everything looked different at night and on foot.

I turned to go back when headlights strobed across the trees. A car was winding toward me on the main road. Primal instinct took over. I did not want to be caught in those lights out here in the dark by myself. Three quick steps and I disappeared into the woods like a forest animal.

Crouching in the thick brush was a prickly experience, but I kept my head down and turned off the flashlight. The sound of the engine grew closer and tires hissed on wet pavement. The car slowed as it approached the shrouded entrance to Gamma Rose's driveway. I couldn't see the vehicle itself, but the headlamps were high off the ground, like a pickup or SUV. Which described nearly every vehicle in these parts.

It slowed even more—and turned into the driveway. Headlights flashed across the brush where I was hidden. I averted my white face while the vehicle rolled past me toward the house. Who in the world would be coming here at night? And why?

I had left Gamma there alone and helpless. When the taillights rounded a curve, I burst from the woods and jogged after them in the darkness.

The dooryard had no sentinel light and I hadn't thought to leave a lamp on inside the house. I saw now that vehicle was an older model SUV, a dark color or black. It stopped behind my car beneath overhanging trees, a shapeless hulk in the shadows. The driver killed the engine and I ducked behind the trunk of an oak, waiting for the interior lights to blink on when someone got out. I wanted to see the visitor before he saw me.

But nothing happened. Whoever it was just sat there.

Where was my shotgun when I needed it? All I had was this weenie flashlight.

For several breathless seconds everything was still, even the creatures of the woods. I tried to make a plan. What would I do if nobody got out? Approach the darkened car? Race for the front door and lock myself in? And what would I do if someone did get out?

Then the vehicle started up again. It made a slow three-point turn and came back down the driveway toward my hiding place with the lights blazing. I stayed out of sight, my heart pounding. What the heck was going on? I didn't stick my head up until the SUV was safely past.

When the taillights slipped out of sight, I jogged to the house, let myself in without turning on the lamp, and locked the door. There was a small back porch off the kitchen and the only lock on that door was an old-fashioned slide bolt that fastened on the inside of the doorjamb. I shot the bolt across knowing that one good kick from outside would splinter the wood.

I closed the curtains and turned on a lamp. Gamma Rose was sleeping in the same position as when I'd left. I stood in her doorway and took deep breaths.

Stop being paranoid. Nothing has changed. There is no real danger. Someone probably turned down the wrong driveway.

When the kitchen phone shrilled in the quiet house, I nearly peed my pants. My shin cracked on a low table and I hopped to the phone.

The voice on the other end was male and vaguely familiar. "Miss Morrell?"

Who knew I was here?

"It's Jake with Ozark Shepherd. Everything okay there?"

"Jake!" My shoulders went slack. "Yes, we're fine. Why?"

"The storm knocked out the phone lines east of you, and I was checking to make sure you had service."

"Apparently we do. Thanks." I was still out of breath and not ready to turn loose of a friendly voice. "Greta called earlier. She's coming tomorrow at ten and will give Gamma Rose her bath."

"Yes, I spoke with her." He paused. "You sound a little shaky. Is Miss Rose okay?"

"She is." I exhaled. "Somebody drove up to the house tonight. They stopped in the yard for a minute, then turned around and left."

"Probably lost. It's easy to do on those roads, especially at night."

I felt ridiculous. I am not a person who's easily spooked. Usually.

"What kind of car was it?" he asked.

"I'm not sure. It was too dark to tell." And I was cowering in the brush.

"Do you want me to drive out and stay with you for a while?"

"No, that's not necessary," I said. "I don't know why I'm so jumpy this evening."

"I do. You're way out in the woods with someone who might die at any time."

"Yeah. There's that."

"Next time I come, I'll stay with Miss Rose so you can get away for a while. Maybe drive into Madison. Take a break."

"That sounds really good, actually," I admitted.

I could hear his smile. "Call if you need something, or just want to talk. See you soon."

After I'd hung up, I sat cross-legged on the lumpy sofa with the window open and practiced meditation. The bones of the old house crackled and running water whispered from the woods. I sat for twenty minutes but couldn't attain Zen, so I lay on my back and made a mental list of my worries and questions, which progressed from logical to bizarre as the hours ticked by.

1. What would I need to do when Gamma Rose died? This was major and I hadn't thought it through. Quite likely, it would be up to me to settle her affairs. Did she own the house and the land where it sat? Did she have important papers somewhere—deeds, a bank account, a will?

2. I had to talk to Drew. Soon. He never did anything without a reason, and whatever his reason for wanting to see me, I needed to know.

3. What happened to my grandmother Pesha? Where had she gone when she ran away? How long had she lived? Somebody had to know.

4. Was I attracted to Jake? Would Gamma Rose's chickens return from the woods and stalk me? Did Donald Trump and Conan O'Brien have the same barber?

At some point I drifted off and awoke at first light, groggy and disoriented. When I remembered where I was, I vowed to deal with two problems that day. I would phone Drew, and I would talk with Gamma Rose about putting her affairs in order.

One of the other questions resolved itself before breakfast. From the dooryard came the unmistakable sound of clucking. Gamma heard it, too, and she wanted to see which of the hens had returned. I rolled her chair to the front door and she sat there watching one bronze and one black hen scratch through the feed, talking in low, curled voices.

"It's Penny and Midnight." Wrinkles pleated around her smile. "They'll eat right out of your hand."

Not my hand, they wouldn't. But maybe we'd have fresh eggs.

Meanwhile, I made oatmeal for breakfast again, along with good strong coffee. While Gamma Rose's mind was clear, I eased into the subject of what to do about her property after she was gone.

"There are some things I probably should know," I said. "Like, do you have a will?"

"I made one a long time ago. Hired a lawyer so it would be good and legal."

"Smart. Where do you keep important papers like that?"

She pointed to the pound cake Jake had left us and I cut her a piece. Oatmeal and cake for breakfast. What's wrong with that?

Her voice sounded like sandpaper this morning. "In a lock box at the bank."

"Really? In a gadžo bank?"

"Why not? Gadže are better businessmen."

I smiled and topped up our coffee. "Is there anything you want me to know about or take care of for you?"

She thought this over. "I don't remember what else is in that box. We should go to the bank and look through it."

I imagined trying to get her into the car, then into the bank and back again without a mishap. "Is there any way I could bring the contents here, so we could take our time and go through it together?"

She shrugged. "Maybe. I think I put your name on the card."

"Really? You listed me to have access to the lock box?"

"The lawyer said I should have two people. You're my only kin."

Unless Pesha was alive. Obviously, Gamma Rose didn't think so.

"I'll need your key to the lock box," I said. "Can you tell me where it is?"

She frowned. "The silverware drawer. Or maybe in the red rooster."

There was no key in the drawer. "The red rooster," I said, looking around at the chicken tchotchkes.

She pointed to a cabinet and I opened the door. At the very back was a rusty tin canister marked Red Rooster Tea. I held it up and she nodded.

Gamma Rose's hidey hole. I pried off the lid and dumped the contents on the table. A ruby ring that might have been real or fake. A souvenir book of matches with Gypsy Rose Club printed on the cover. And no fewer than eight metal keys. There was also a miniature cardboard envelope closed with a snap. On the outside was printed "F&M Bank of Madison. Box no. 35."

"Okay," I said. "We'll do that soon."

The morning was clear and sunny, and I dried off our outdoor chairs so she could sit in the yard and watch the chickens. I was getting braver about helping her move around. She was so slight I could hold her up easily. Her bones felt hollow as a bird's.

Yellow leaves floated down from the tallest trees. Penny and Midnight migrated to Gamma Rose's feet but wisely avoided me. The birds were obviously her pets, and it pleased me to see how much she enjoyed them. Recognizing a photo op, I quickly retrieved the colorful silk scarf from her bedroom and grabbed my cell phone.

"I'd like to take your picture. Is that okay?"

A crooked smile. "Okay."

I spread the scarf around her shoulders, tucked the ends into her hands, and stepped back to frame the shot. The hens milled around her chair, Penny's copper feathers picking up the color of metallic threads in the scarf.

"I'm as pretty as you are," Gamma said to the chickens, and I caught her smile at the perfect moment. It was a picture I would treasure the rest of my life.

I held the cell phone screen to show her. "It's too little," she said and pushed it away. We had left her glasses in the house.

Greta arrived promptly at ten. She greeted Gamma Rose like a friend rather than a patient. Dimpled elbows showed below the sleeves of her flowered smock as she unloaded an oxygen machine from her car.

"I'll set it up before I go and show you how it works," she said.

"Hmm." I remembered the aide at the hospice facility who claimed Gamma Rose removed the oxygen tube whenever they put it in her nose.

I helped my great-granny indoors while Greta lugged the machine. She checked Gamma's heartbeat and blood pressure, then laid her out on the bed and began gently exercising her arms and legs to improve circulation. After that, a bath was on the agenda.

"Do you mind if I go for a walk while you're with Gamma Rose?" I asked. I wanted to exorcize my unseemly fear from the previous night by exploring the woods in daylight.

"Sure, fresh air will be good for you," Greta said. "I'll be here at least another hour."

Gamma Rose had her eyes squeezed shut, doing her best to ignore the nurse's hands on her body. "I'll be back soon," I told her, but she didn't respond.

I coerced my frizzy hair into a pony tail and nabbed the walking stick I'd seen propped behind the kitchen door. It was natural wood, shaped and smoothed by water or time. It felt good in my hand. I liked the idea that at a younger age Gamma Rose had used the stick to go walking in these hills. If I saved nothing else from Gamma's house, I was going to claim this as my heirloom.

Sunshine and cool air improved my mood. If I could whistle, I would have done so as I set out through the trees behind the house. It would be rugged going, all uphill with no path, a welcome challenge. I seriously needed some exercise. My ears would lead me to that Ozark stream.

A hundred feet up the slope I hit the wall. More specifically, an eight-foot-high chain-link fence. What was that doing here? I'm opposed to fencing wild places without a good reason because it cuts off wildlife from their natural paths. The terrain here looked too steep and woodsy for cattle, so I doubted the need for such a barrier.

Determined to climb the hill, I spotted a gate off to my left and worked my way toward it. Judging by the rust and vines that clung to the wire, the fence had been here a long time. And it wasn't meant for cattle. This was an anti-people fence. It had barbed wire on top like a prison yard and the gate was padlocked. Why? Most people around here didn't even lock their houses.

By now I was sweaty and frustrated. I picked up a stone that required two hands and bashed it against the rusted lock. The lock held, but one link of the rusty chain that looped through it gaped open. I bashed it again and worked the chain loose, justifying my vandalism by telling myself I was Gamma Rose's only heir. I had a right to see the property.

Because of trees and underbrush the gate would open only a foot. I squeezed through and used the walking stick to bushwhack my way upward. I hadn't expected the ground vegetation to be so thick among all these trees. Only about a quarter of their leaves had fallen, and I recognized black oak and hickory and honey locust. Others I'd never seen. Goldenrod and wild asters bloomed in dappled patches among tangled grasses and vines.

The morning was windless and gnats targeted my eyes. I should have put on bug spray. And brought water. Even so, I inhaled the rich autumn scents and enjoyed the pleasant burn of muscles too long unused.

My ears strained to hear the stream, but it didn't sound any closer. Finally I emerged into a treeless space created by an outcropping of cherty rocks. I scrambled onto the highest spot and sat to catch my breath. If I found that stream, would it be safe to drink?

Below me through the trees I glimpsed the cabin's roof, camouflaged by moss and branches. I checked the time on my cell phone to see how long I'd been gone. Almost half an hour. I'd have to start back without finding the stream. Up here with a view of the open sky, the reception icon on my phone showed two bars. Would it actually work?

Drew's mobile number had been programmed into my phone for a long time, though I hadn't called it since he'd accepted a good job offer and gone back to New York. I tapped the number and waited, my pulse clogdancing in my throat. I had no idea what to say when I heard his voice for the first time in months.

Nothing original, that's for sure. "Drew? It's Chantalene."

"Chantalene."

I savored the pleasure I heard in his voice.

"Hold on a sec and let me step outside, okay?" I heard him excuse himself, then rustling, and a door close. "Sorry. I was in a meeting."

"Bad timing is my specialty."

"You did me a favor. It was boring."

"I got your letter," I said. "I'm sorry I took so long to respond."

"I was getting ready to phone Thelma."

I laughed. "She'd have loved that. But she's watching my place while I'm in Arkansas with my great-grandmother. The doctor says Gamma Rose is dying."

"Oh… I'm sorry to hear that."

"She has no other family. I can't leave her alone."

"Of course." He hesitated. "When you get back, I'd like to come see you."

"I'd like that, too. But I have no idea how long it will be. Is there anything you want to talk about over the phone?"

He sighed, and I heard a chair squeak. I pictured him at a desk in one of those Manhattan high-rises. Maybe a cubicle where if he stood up he could almost see the Statue of Liberty through the window of his boss's corner office. Or maybe, by now, he was the boss with the corner office.

"I need to see you in person," he said.

Need to. I couldn't stand it. "Drew, are you getting married? If you are, please just tell me."

"No." He gave a sort of half laugh, but when he spoke again I could tell he was serious. "Not unless you've changed your mind."

I teetered on my rocky perch. "Drew," was all I could say.

On the phone I heard a muffled knock and a female voice. Perhaps his assistant summoning him back to the meeting. "Two minutes," he said, away from the phone. Then he was back with me. "Can I get a flight to where you are now?"

"Crooked Dog Creek, Arkansas?"

"Maybe not. Anywhere near Little Rock?"

"About two hundred miles north of that, and it's hard to find. Why don't I call you when I know I'm headed back home?"

"Will you?"

"I promise. This is my cell, so now you have my number. I could come pick you up at the airport in Oklahoma City."

"That would be great." He paused again. "I've missed you."

The lump in my throat almost prevented my answering. "That goes both ways."

After we hung up, I sat on the sun-warmed rock, thrilled and miserable. I still loved him. But he had always wanted kids, and he would be a great dad. It wasn't right for him to give that up for a woman who might be gone in a handful of years.

I crashed back down the mountain and spent too much time trying to re-find the gate. Greta would be ready to leave and wondering where I was. When I arrived, breathless and sweating, she had set up the oxygen unit and had the cannula in place in Gamma Rose's nose. I bet that was a struggle and was glad I missed it.

Greta showed me how to operate the machine. "She doesn't have to wear it when she's up and around, but she ought to keep it on whenever she's in bed. It will ease her breathing and help keep her mind clear."

"Got it."

When Greta had gone, I went back to Gamma's room. She was tired from being "mauled by that nurse" and refused any lunch except the protein shake. I held the aluminum can for her while she took tiny sips with a straw.

"Gamma Rose, why is that tall fence around your property on the mountain?"

She frowned as if she didn't understand.

"I went up the hill on my walk, but it's all fenced off. Why?"

"Trespassers," she said in a growl.

"Who, kids having a keg party?"

"Nosey people. Leaving their trash around."

"So the fence wasn't there when you bought the land?"

"No. I hired someone to get it done."

I could see she was getting sleepy. She pushed the chocolate shake away. I adjusted the cannula in her nose.

"Is there a waterfall up there? It sounded like it, after the rain."

"Don't go up there," she said. "You could fall and get hurt."

"You're sweet to worry, but I'm pretty sure footed. And I'd love to find that stream."

Gamma Rose was frowning now and her voice grew harsh. "Don't go up there. It's a bad place. The mountain is cursed."

"Cursed? How's that?"

But she folded her hands and closed her eyes. She wasn't really asleep, but she was through talking.

SEVEN

JAKE SHOWED UP that afternoon even though he was off the clock. Gamma Rose was napping and I was sitting outdoors, reading with my sunglasses on. He climbed out of his truck and sauntered toward me, smiling.

"How's Miss Rose?"

"Greta worked her over this morning. She's sleeping it off."

"And how's Miss Rose's keeper?"

I gave him a sheepish smile. "Better than last night. Sorry if I sounded spooked. I do appreciate that you called to check on us." I pushed my sunglasses up on my head and motioned toward the second chair.

He sat. "New book?"

"Yeah, I finished the last one. I may have to take you up on letting me borrow one."

"I'll bring a couple tomorrow."

He stretched out his legs and squinted toward the bright sky. In the sunshine I saw lines around his eyes and mouth that I hadn't noticed before. He was older than I'd first thought. He wore it well.

"Let me know whenever you need to get away for a bit. I can stay with Miss Rose. It's one of the services we provide."

I laid the book in my lap. "As a matter of fact, I need to go to her bank in Madison." I checked my watch, but it was already four and Madison was more than half an hour away. "Maybe tomorrow morning?"

"Sure. I'll put it on the schedule."

I finally remembered my manners. "Want something to drink?"

"Ah, no thanks. I have to go. Just wanted to check on you ladies." He stood. "Nine o'clock tomorrow?"

"Perfect. I appreciate it." I had a quick vision of zooming down a civilized street with the radio on, grabbing something unhealthy at a fast-food place. It was pathetic how much I looked forward to it.

Jake climbed into the truck and rolled away slowly, careful not to throw dust in my eyes. What a guy. Maybe he was gay.

I was deep into the climax of Tess Gerritsen's *The Silent Girl* when I thought I heard Gamma Rose's voice. I rushed to her bedroom and stopped at the doorway.

The oxygen machine wheezed its monotonous rhythm. Gamma was reaching out, her eyes focused on empty space toward the foot of the bed. A chill ran through me—zero at the bone.

I placed my hand on her shoulder and spoke softly, hoping not to startle her. "Gamma Rose? It's all right. I'm here." She continued to stare, her eyes glassy. "What do you see?"

Her voice rasped. "He comes back to haunt me."

"Who is it?" I waited. "Is it Yoors? Your husband?"

Her mouth worked but she didn't answer. Then her arms dropped and her eyes closed as if someone had turned off a switch. She lay so still that once again I thought she was gone. I laid two fingers on her neck and felt a weak pulse.

I stayed by her bed the rest of the afternoon. By her own account their marriage was congenial, so why would her husband's spirit haunt her? And if not Yoors, then who?

WHEN GAMMA AWOKE, she seemed fairly lucid. I didn't ask if she remembered the incident. It seemed clear that she wasn't fully conscious during those episodes. When we made a trip to the bathroom, I could tell she was weaker.

Afterward, I helped her settle into the geri chair in the kitchen. Spaghetti marinara and green beans were on the supper menu. While the pasta boiled, I told her about Jake staying the next morning while I went to the bank. She nodded agreement, though she might not remember by tomorrow. Her hand trembled when she tried to feed herself. She took two bites of spaghetti, then shook her head, refusing more. She asked for water.

After I washed the dishes, she asked again to sit outdoors. I was not going to deny her any wish.

Her breath came short as we navigated to our positions in the front yard. I spread a blanket across her lap, and we sat and listened.

I had developed a genuine affection toward my great-grandmother, and I took a moment to mourn the impending loss. I'd had no family for many years and keenly hoped this would not be our last evening together.

Early stars peppered the darkening sky. Penny and Midnight had gone to roost. A squirrel vaulted through the treetops to its leafy nest. The woods exhaled and grew still or I might not have noticed a dark shape moving through the trees.

Gamma Rose saw the movement, too, and hissed one word. Zabella. It might have been a name or a Gypsy curse.

The shape materialized into a woman in a long skirt that rocked with each step. A black shawl covered her head and shoulders. When at last she came into the open, I recognized the granite face I'd seen twice in Gamma's room at the hospice. The woman with the dry-ice voice who had brought the scarf.

Zabella. She had made her act of contrition and been forgiven. Why was she here? I didn't want her presence upsetting my fragile great-grandmother. I glanced at Gamma Rose and her expression surprised me. She looked—grateful? Or maybe relieved.

It was suddenly clear to me that these two women had history. They were bound together by shared experience or misery, grudging accomplices in the march of old age.

Zabella swayed into the yard, steadying herself with an ebony cane. She stopped in front of Gamma's chair and they looked at each other, unsmiling. After a moment Gamma Rose said, "Daughter, get this old woman a chair."

It took a second to realize she was talking to me. I rose quickly and gestured to our visitor. "Please. Take mine."

I wasn't about to go inside for another chair and miss something. I sat cross-legged on the ground near Gamma Rose. Zabella eased herself onto the chair and held the cane between her knees. Its carved knob was a tiger's head with golden eyes that winked in the moonlight. From my seat on the ground, the old women were silhouettes against a spangled sky.

The whole woodland seemed to wait. Finally, in her crushed voice, Zabella spoke.

"Are you suffering, Rose?"

Gamma Rose was silent several beats. She tapped her chest with a curled hand. "The wounds and indignities of a long life."

There was another long silence, then Gamma puffed air through her lips. "I'm straddling two horses with one behind. The worst part is knowing that I'm losing my mind."

Gamma Rose had never voiced a complaint to me. I was surprised she would confide this to someone who wasn't family. Thelma once told me that we all need a witness to our lives. Someone who's known us forever, the good, the bad, and the ugly, the myriad experiences that made us who we are. Perhaps this old Gypsy was Gamma Rose's witness.

"Don't worry," Zabella said. "If you say something you shouldn't, no one will believe you." She cackled like one of the yard hens and Gamma smirked.

Another pause. "Did you ever hear from Ian?" Gamma asked.

A cricket grew old in the silence and stopped fiddling.

"I heard he died," Zabella said.

Gamma Rose nodded. "His lungs were never strong."

In the next silence I asked, "Who's Ian?" and was soundly ignored.

A shadow swooped through the clearing on silent wings, not three feet above their heads, and stole my breath. Branches shivered as the owl came to rest and fixed us with a primeval gaze. Shivers ran over my whole body, but the two old women ignored the specter in the trees.

"And her? Is she alive?" Gamma said.

"I know nothing."

Who was she? The owl's hoot, unbelievably loud this close, pebbled my skin. I kept quiet and waited.

"So you'll be buried next to Yoors," Zabella said.

"Where else."

Zabella tipped her head toward me ever so slightly. "What about this one?"

Gamma Rose made a low sound that might have been approval. "You don't have to worry about her."

Zabella heaved a sigh. "Umm. Soon we'll both be past worrying."

She arose without warning. Palming the tiger-headed cane, Zabella rocked into the night with no word of good-bye. The owl arose, as well, with powerful flaps of its wings. It sailed over the house toward the fenced mountain, vanishing into the night.

I watched Zabella go, a dozen questions alive in my brain. Before I could pose even one, Gamma Rose issued my orders.

"Help me to bed now."

Small groans escaped from her throat as I practically carried her into the house. She was so weak I asked her nothing. Her eyes were closed before her head settled on the pillow.

That night my sleep was haunted by winged phantoms and the whisper of water.

THE NEXT MORNING she seemed a little better. Whatever genetic defect we might share was clearly no match for my redoubtable great-grandmother. I reminded her that Jake was coming to stay with her while I went to the bank. "Unless you'd rather I didn't go today."

"You go." Her smile was mischievous. "That boy is handsome and he brings cake."

The handsome boy arrived right on time and an hour later I had located the F&M Bank of Madison. When I'd phoned ahead, I had spoken with a Mr. Barrington, who recognized Gamma Rose's name immediately. Despite its prosperity, Madison was still a small town where most people knew each other's business. Especially the banker.

He greeted me in the lobby. Ben Barrington was a caricature of an old-style banker, plump with a halo of dark hair around his bald head. He wore a rumpled navy suit, a red bow tie, and the scent of thick cigars.

"Miss Morrell," he said when I introduced myself. He shook my hand. "Please sit down. How is your great-grandmother?"

"The doctor says she doesn't have long. Congestive heart failure."

"Sorry to hear that. She's been a customer for many years."

"She said her important papers are in a safe deposit box here and my name is on the list for access." I laid the key on the edge of the desk. "We want to go through them together while there's still time."

He nodded thoughtfully. "Wise thing to do. I'll get our matching key and let you in myself." He pressed an intercom button and gave instructions.

"I'll need to see some ID," he said. "Protocol, you know."

I showed him my driver's license. He glanced at it, then leaned back in his chair.

"Your great-grandmother chose to live simply and keep to herself. She could have been a wealthy woman."

"Excuse me?"

"She probably didn't tell you that, did she?" He leaned forward, obviously enjoying the story I didn't know. "Years ago, an old prospector donated some ancient petroglyphs to the state historical museum. He said he'd found them on that mountain behind her house when he was just a kid. He claimed there were more in a cave up there. The curators went nuts, but Missus Tsura wouldn't let anybody on the property to check out the site." He smiled as if this was a great joke on them.

"How would that make her wealthy?" I asked.

"When news of the petroglyphs filtered through the archeological grapevine, a rich collector from Florida made a generous offer to buy her land so his museum colleagues could explore. Very generous." He nodded, his eyebrows lifting. "She could have moved to town or a retirement resort—anywhere she wanted. But she wouldn't sell."

"Wow." I was struck dumb by this bit of information.

He sat back in his chair. "I assume you'll inherit."

"I have no idea."

His assistant came in with a ring of keys, the proper one singled out. "Thank you, Cherise," he said. Then to me, "Shall we?"

Mr. Barrington led me to a windowless room walled with fireproof drawers, a mausoleum for treasured documents. Using both our keys, he opened drawer number thirty-five, withdrew the heavy box, and set it on a high table for me. He returned my key, took his, and left.

I lifted the metal lid of the box. The top item was an ivory envelope bearing the logo of a law firm. Probably her will. I laid it aside. Beneath that was the abstract for her twenty acres in Marion County, thick with history. It would have to be brought up to date when the land passed to a new owner. Maybe the abstract would shed some light on my family history.

I slid both items into the World Wildlife tote bag I'd brought with me. The only thing left in the drawer was a sealed brown envelope. It bore no writing or label. Curious, I popped loose the old glue, undid the clasp, and dumped out the contents. A handful of black-and-white photos fell onto the table.

The same young woman appeared in each shot, sometimes with others. She had crow-black hair, a slim build, and eyes that challenged the camera. In two photos she was holding an infant. But the picture that stopped my breath showed her posed alone in what must have been her wedding dress. She was not smiling and there was trouble in her eyes.

It was like looking at a time-travel photo of myself at that age, after my parents had died. "You look like Pesha," Gamma Rose had said. "When you came in, I thought it was her."

I hadn't found any pictures of Pesha among my great-grandmother's box of old photos because they were all here. I was looking at the missing link in my mitochondrial history.

I examined each photo again, wondering where she went after fleeing the closed society of the Romani. Gamma Rose called her headstrong, and I could see that in her eyes. Maybe she had good reasons. Another way we were alike. If I confronted Gamma Rose with these photos, would she tell me more about Pesha?

I slid the photos back into the envelope and realized there was something else inside. I pulled out a letter, addressed in a feminine hand. There was no return address. My fingers jittered as I opened it.

Dear Mama,

I am sorry for running away, but I cannot stay with that beng. I won't live with a man who hits. One of us would surely kill the other. I will come back for the baby as soon as it is safe. I beg you to take good care of her. I know you will.

Love, Pesha.

The baby she spoke of was my mother, the infant pictured with her in the other photos. I shuffled back to examine my mother's infant face.

Had Pesha died from the genetic defect before she could return? Maybe the husband she called a devil found her and exacted revenge. Or maybe Pesha, a mother too young at seventeen, simply slipped into another life and abandoned her child.

I looked for a postmark on the envelope. It was hand-stamped, dated October 1963. The town name was smeared but it might have been Springfield, and the state was definitely Missouri. Pesha had run north.

Maybe there was some record of her there—a rented house, a place of employment. Or maybe it was just too long ago. I didn't even know her married name. Would she have reverted to her maiden name of Tsura? She might have pretended to be married to the young man who helped her run away, whose name I didn't know. Even a detective couldn't follow such an old trail with so little information.

I looked again at the portrait of my grandmother and felt a connection spanning the years. Those troubled eyes would haunt me until I learned her fate. I slid the photos into my bag, returned the metal box to its cave, and left the bank. It was time I asked Gamma Rose some questions, even if I had to explain why Pesha's lifespan was so important to me.

EIGHT

ON THE WAY back to Gamma Rose's house, I stopped for fast food and some groceries. When I arrived, Jake met me at the door, his face somber.

"She wouldn't rouse enough to eat any lunch," he said, keeping his voice low. "She's winding down. I don't think she can last much longer. This will probably be harder for you than for her." He took the grocery sack from my hands.

My throat caught. I tossed the tote bag on the sofa and went to her bedside.

Her cheeks were sunken, her breathing shallow. I hoped Jake was right about it being easier for her than for me. It felt selfish, but I mourned not only my great-grandmother but the answers I needed from her. I knelt by the bed and took her hand.

"I'm home, Gamma Rose. I love you." I didn't know if she could hear me.

"Would you like me to stay?" Jake whispered from the doorway. "I could make arrangements."

I straightened and wiped the corners of my eyes. "I appreciate the offer, but we'll be okay." I wanted to be alone with her in her last moments, a sentiment that surprised me more than a little. "I know you have other clients who need you."

"If you're sure."

I nodded. I knew Jake was a compassionate person, but his hug still surprised me. I'd never been a hugger, maybe because of my rocky childhood. I stood stiffly with my hands between us. It felt weird having his arms around me, though it lasted only seconds. I wondered if hugging was standard procedure for a hospice worker. He was strong but gentle, and he smelled good.

After he left, the house suddenly felt chilly. A north wind had ushered in low-hanging clouds, and the brisk change caught me by surprise. The sky looked more like winter than fall. I closed the living room window and checked on Gamma Rose. She was sleeping with no signs of distress or unseen visitors.

In the kitchen, I made oolong tea with honey and laid out the materials from the bank on the kitchen table—the abstract, Pesha's photos and letter, and the fat envelope bearing the return address of a law firm in Madison. I opened that one first and unfolded several legal-sized pages. It was titled "Last Will and Testament of Gamma Rose Tsura." The words brought unexpected tears to my eyes.

Sipping from my designated mug, I scanned the legalese that introduced the document and turned the page to a listing of her property. There wasn't much. Her bank accounts, one savings and one checking, were left to me. The house and one acre, together with all household goods and the dead car in the side yard, also went to me. Twenty acres with a legal description I presumed to be the mountain slope behind the house, she had willed to Zabella Mallosh.

Zabella? Why? I felt sure it was the same reason she'd warned me not to explore up there. What was the great secret those two old women shared? Was this bequest meant to cement the collusion between them, to ensure that what they knew would not be revealed? I had no claim on that land, nor did I want it. But more and more I suspected the secret it hid had to do with Pesha's disappearance. I didn't understand how Zabella was connected.

Back in Gamma's bedroom, the oxygen machine heaved and sighed. I straightened the cannula in her nose and tucked the tube behind her ear where it had come undone.

She opened her eyes and I smiled. "Hi. It's me again."

"You're still here," she said.

I reached for her hand. "Yes, I am."

I sat in the chair beside her bed. "Gamma Rose, I need to ask you some things. What's on that land behind the house? It has something to do with Pesha, doesn't it?"

Her breath rattled. I felt like a monster but pressed on. "I need to know about her. It's important."

Finally she managed a raspy whisper. "If only Yoors had lived. She listened to her father."

My heart skittered. "I found the letter she wrote you. She promised to come back for her baby. Why didn't she?"

Her eyes closed and I was afraid the moment of lucidity was lost, but she spoke again. "She did. He found her and dragged her back."

"Her husband?"

"Tobar." The pink mole appeared in a dry effort to spit on his name. "I was wrong to make her marry him."

"What happened to Pesha after that?"

Tears formed at the corners of her eyes. "I sent her away. My beautiful daughter."

A soft keening rose from her open mouth. I kissed the back of her hand. "Don't cry, Gamma. It's all right. I won't question you anymore."

The mewling dissolved into shallow breaths and her hand went slack. Her eyes closed. I pulled the quilt up to her chin and left the room.

Still feeling like an ogre, I paced three figure eights through the living room furniture. I was too close to finding out what happened to my grandmother to stop now. Finally, I made a decision.

Jake answered his cell on the third ring. He couldn't have been more than halfway back to Madison by now.

"I need your help," I said. "Can you elder sit for a while again tomorrow?"

"Let me check with the office. I'm sure we can work something out. I'll let you know what time."

Thank goodness he didn't ask questions. Gamma Rose wasn't going to tell me what was hidden on the mountainside. I had to figure it out while she could still explain whatever I might find. The only way to do that was to search the whole twenty acres.

JAKE ARRIVED AT one-thirty the next afternoon and I met him in the front yard. I was wearing my red hoodie and carrying a bottle of water and Gamma Rose's walking stick.

He frowned. "You're going on a walk?"

Clearly he didn't feel justified in changing his schedule so I could take a hike. "It's important, I promise. I'll explain later, but I need to get moving so I can get back before dark."

His eyebrows lifted, but he looked more curious than upset. "Whatever. Don't get lost."

He went indoors to see Gamma Rose, and I set out toward the woods behind the house. Working my way upward, I aimed for the gate I'd discovered the day before yesterday. It seemed more like a week ago.

More leaves had fallen overnight and it was easier to see the fortress-like fence through the trees. I found the gate easily, squeezed through, and continued my climb.

Spurred by adrenaline, I kept a steady pace up the incline, passing the rocky spot where I had stopped to phone Drew. I wished he were here now. I was plowing through thick woods alone and didn't know where I was going. Twenty acres is a lot of territory when you're on foot, but at least the fence would give me a perimeter. My plan was to start at the top left corner and zig-zag my way down in horizontal lines like a search-party grid.

Meanwhile, clouds gathered overhead pushed by a chilly wind. The ceiling blurred into a gray mist. My sweatshirt was warm but not waterproof, and the soles of my sneakers would be slick if it started to rain. I hadn't considered bringing rain gear on a trip to the Ozarks.

Working my way upward, I stayed close to the left fence line where the brush was less dense. It took a long time. The property seemed deeper than it was wide, but that perception might be skewed by the fact that it was all uphill. I couldn't see the mountaintop for the trees, and nothing hinted of an approaching summit.

I was winded by the time I glimpsed a fence cutting across my path some fifty feet ahead. This had to be the back edge of Gamma Rose's land. I reached the chain-link borderline and leaned against it to catch my breath. Altitude was not a factor in these squat mountains, but exertion was. I took a swig of water and looked through the fence. The land kept rising. Gamma's tract did not reach the summit.

Now that I was standing still, I heard the burble of water. When I faced downhill, the sound seemed to come from above, and also to my left.

I moved about twenty-five feet downhill and began walking a horizontal line across the slope, parallel with the back fence. I focused mostly on the ground, scanning left to right, but occasionally looking upward as well. When you don't know what you're looking for, it's hard to know where to look.

The earthy smell of autumn hung around me. The aroma of burning leaves wafted up the rise. I couldn't see the smoke but recognized the scent. Counting paces to estimate the distance, I tramped over fallen trees and around patches of poison ivy, drooping from an early frost. Wild grape vines looped into upper branches. My progress silenced the birds except for a pair of cheeky crows flying overhead. In a glimpse of clouded sky, I saw a vulture circling, searching for food. Its eerie silhouette inspired me to keep moving.

At ninety-four paces I came upon the water. It was a shallow stream, about two feet wide, that meandered down a diagonal path without much speed or voice. Was this miniature creek what I had been hearing every day? Mildly disappointed, I vaulted it with the aid of my walking stick and moved on.

Now the water noise was both behind and in front of me. I'd gone two hundred thirty paces before I came across the second fork of the stream. This one was wider and swift enough that I had to search along the bank for a place to cross. I stood on a rock beside the water and watched it boil over rounded stones and disappear into the trees. Its path angled toward the smaller stream. If both streams maintained their direction, they would converge at some lower point and form a significant flow. I was guessing that convergence was what I'd been hearing during my wakeful nights. It sounded like a small waterfall.

My impulse was to follow the stream down to that meeting place, but that meant I'd have to abandon my grid and I wouldn't have surveyed the whole twenty acres. I could very well miss something important. Instead I crossed the water, stepping on dry stones in the streambed, but my final leap fell short of my aim. My wet shoe made a disgusting sound as I trudged on.

It was hard to tell if I was walking a straight line or veering too far down the slope. The brush was thicker here, and I'd lost sight of the fence at the top. All I could do was keep moving forward, watching for anything out of the ordinary. Or snakes.

Ahead, a rocky ridge rose against the clouded sky. Without tree cover, yellowish limestone caught the light and I saw a promontory like the prow of a ship jutting from the hillside. I bushwhacked through the undergrowth and arrived at an area of cherty rocks at its base.

I looked up. Wind whispered around forbidding rock formations at the top, and in places the crags rose nearly perpendicular to the earth. Among the stones, sparse tufts of weeds and grass were browned by frost. The place was remarkably still, as if something here demanded silence.

A dense cloud passed over the summit and I felt its shadow in my bones. I wondered if this was where the petroglyphs had been found, if they really existed. It seemed possible, though I saw nothing that looked like a cave. If I could get up there, the promontory would provide a bird's-eye view of the entire twenty acres, and perhaps a clue to where I should look next.

It wouldn't be an easy climb. I was doubly glad to have Gamma Rose's walking stick for balance. I used it like a third leg as I began to navigate the rocky approach. Turning an ankle was a possibility I did not take lightly. How long would it take someone to come looking, let alone find me, if I wasn't able to walk?

The bluffs became steeper as I ascended, stepping from the top of one foothold to the next. The fissures between boulders grew deeper and wider, and I dared not jump across. If I lost my footing, I could easily break a leg. I shinnied down one rock formation and scrambled on all fours up the next. My jeans were white with rock dust, my palms scraped and raw. I was still a long way from the summit.

The walking stick was now a hindrance instead of a help, something else to hold onto. But I wasn't about to give it up. I would need it to keep from falling when I came back down. Especially since fat raindrops had started to spatter the rocks and smack my face. If the rain picked up, these rocks would get slick.

But I couldn't turn back now. I was nearing the highest point and determined to know what I could see from there.

The drops kept coming but didn't increase. When I finally reached the top, the walking stick was my friend again. I eased out onto a flat boulder and surveyed acres of oaks, sycamores, and hemlock in shades of green and gold and rust. Downhill a good distance, the two streams came together and formed a vigorous flow, wide enough that I caught a glimpse of white water. Then it leveled out and disappeared, angling away from Gamma Rose's land. This must be the stream I had crossed on the paved road from Madison.

The view was impressive and worth the climb. I took a few moments to enjoy it, but I didn't see anything valuable or mysterious that might have induced Gamma Rose to put up that prison-like fence. I sharpened my focus and turned 360 degrees, slowly scrutinizing each rise and fall of the land, every niche and aberration. I searched for something manmade or incongruent with the Ozark landscape. Something that didn't belong.

Dogs barked in the distance, maybe hounds. I saw nothing but rocks, water, and trees.

I huffed, my shoulders drooping. The raindrops were coming smaller and faster, a predictor of more to come. Better get down from here before the rocks turned slick or lightning picked me off.

Easing my way down from the promontory, I saw a deep and narrow crevasse between the cliff where I stood and the next. I stepped closer and peered over the edge, the bottoms of my feet prickling. It must have been thirty feet straight down. Something whitish lay at the bottom. Something long and thin, and much smoother than the dead branches I'd hiked across. Something that didn't belong.

I lay flat on my belly and scooted closer to the edge, which rounded precipitously toward the drop. I removed my sunglasses and squinted into the abyss.

The object looked far too much like a thigh bone. Not long enough for a horse or cow, too long for a coyote or bobcat. Just right for a human being.

I inched farther until I could see the bottom of the fissure. There were other, smaller bones. One was flat and cupped, like a pelvis. Definitely not an animal. And a few feet away, wedged between two stones, a rounded white object about the size of a human skull.

My stomach heaved. It had never occurred to me I might be looking for a body.

Could this be my grandmother Pesha? If not, then who? I had to know and I was certain Gamma Rose had the answer. There was no reason for that prison-like fence around her property except to conceal these bones. What happened on this mountain, and why?

I could not retrieve any of the bones on my own. Even if I managed to get down there safely, I couldn't get back up. This was a job for the local police and a rock-climbing specialist. I lay with my cheek on the damp rock, breathing through my mouth, rain pelting my face and soaking into my hoodie, and waited for my knees to stop quaking.

Carefully, I rose to my feet on the wet surface, steadying myself with the walking stick. I straightened my back and took a few deep breaths, assessing the least dangerous path of descent. I had taken only one step when a loud crack echoed off the rocks and down the valley.

My foot slipped and I dropped to my knees, thinking at first of thunder. But this was a steady rain, not a thunderstorm. That sound was a rifle shot.

I sprawled face down on the limestone. Where had it come from? Should I stay flat, or slide ass-over-teakettle down the rocks? I was pretty sure there was no hunting season going on now. That shot was meant for me. It was a miracle I wasn't hit, standing on the highest point in twenty acres in a red jacket.

I was moderately skilled with a rifle and even I would not have missed that shot. Maybe the shooter didn't intend to kill me. It could have been a warning. Don't meddle in local business or you'll wind up like those bones. If there was a second shot, though, I'd likely be dead.

I was breathing hard and afraid to stand. Instead I inched along the rock on my belly toward the lower side and began easing myself over the edge, feet first. It was about a six foot slide to the next level, and the friction pushed up my shirt and scraped my stomach. I swore. My walking stick clattered downhill and caught between two rocks. I couldn't use it here anyway, but I would pick it up on my next stop. It was the only thing I had that remotely resembled a weapon.

One more slide and the tops of trees provided some cover. Unless the shooter was on the ground, I was safer here. I figured he must be higher up. From the ground, there was no clear line of sight to top of the rocky ledge where I'd been standing.

Once my feet hit fairly level ground, I lurched pell-mell downhill toward the sound of the mini-waterfall, swinging my stick ahead of me. From the point of the streams' convergence, the gate would be farther down and to the right. I kept my head low, fearing another shot might split the stillness.

None came. Mercifully, the rain had stopped. By the time I made it to the bottom fence and fought my way along it toward the gate, I was scratched, itchy, and panting. My heartbeat had reached escape velocity.

I squeezed through the gate and jogged the rest of the way to the cabin, gasping for each breath. I was dead set on learning what Gamma Rose knew about those bones.

My hand on the doorknob, I stopped short. Something was wrong.

Jake's pickup was not in the yard.

I pushed into the house. "Jake? You here?" No sign of him and no answer.

I rushed to Gamma Rose's bedroom. She lay motionless with her eyes closed and hands folded on top of the quilt as if posed. Her face was the color of scorched milk. There was no movement of her chest beneath the cotton gown.

I dropped to my knees beside the bed. "Gamma Rose?" Her hand was flaccid and cold. "No, not yet. Not yet!"

Her cheek felt waxy against my palm. My tears dropped on her sleeve. My great-grandmother was dead. Whatever her secrets were, she was taking them to her grave.

NINE

HOW COULD JAKE have left her to die alone? How could I?

Teary-eyed, I backed out of Gamma Rose's bedroom. From the kitchen phone I called Jake's cell. He didn't answer.

I was on my own with no idea what to do now. Why hadn't I asked the hospice people about the procedure after a death? I hadn't wanted to think about it.

In her vintage phone book, I looked up the number for the county sheriff's office. It was the only thing I could think of. Thank goodness, the sheriff was actually in. His voice sounded like the bass in a barbershop quartet.

"Sheriff Donovan. What can I do for you?"

I explained my situation. He recognized Gamma Rose's name and knew where she lived.

"I'm sorry for your loss." He sounded as if he meant it. "I'll contact the coroner and have him meet me there. It shouldn't take more than an hour."

I didn't think to mention the bones I'd found on the mountain. But those weren't going anywhere. We could deal with them later.

I sat on the front step to wait, my head in my hands. The image of Gamma Rose so pale and still burned inside my eyelids. A hollowness as big as all outdoors swelled inside me. I knew this day was coming, but that didn't mean I was ready. My great-grandmother had so much more to teach me. I missed her already.

After what seemed an eternity, two vehicles arrived in tandem. The sheriff climbed down from a gold Chevy pickup with the county emblem on its side. He was a tall man with a big hat, his face as lined as elephant skin and his eyes pale blue and kind. He approached me with a solemn expression.

"Miss Morrell? Sheriff Donovan. I'm sorry about your grandmother."

I stood and shook his extended hand. "I'm Chantalene. She was my great-grandmother, actually."

"I thought you looked pretty young to be the granddaughter. I've known your great-grandmother for years, but I can't say I knew her well."

I nodded but said nothing. She didn't make friends with gadže.

The coroner was younger than I expected. He carried a black leather bag and the cuffs of his jeans bunched above worn cowboy boots. His plaid shirt was untucked.

"Ben Davis," he said and tipped an invisible hat.

"Doctor Davis."

"It's just Ben. In this state a coroner doesn't have to be an M.D." He looked apologetic and shifted the bag from one hand to the other. "I'm here to certify Ms. Tsura's death."

My head bobbed. I had no words, caught up in a bizarre dream. For an awkward moment the three of us stood there.

Finally, the coroner said, "I'll need to see her body."

My bobble-head bobbled again. I turned and opened the door for them. "She's in the bedroom at the back. It's pretty crowded in there, so if it's okay I'll just wait here."

"Certainly."

Both men disappeared into the dark interior. I sat on the step and wished Drew were here. His steadiness and good sense always made things better. I thought about Thelma and Whippoorwill and Bones and wanted to go home. Then I thought of Jake and imagined beating him with a blunt object. When his employer learned he had deserted us, he was toast. I took some consolation in that.

The men's subdued voices drifted through the open door, but I couldn't tell what they were saying. After a while the sheriff came out and I moved aside to let him pass. He stood on the damp ground in front of me.

His voice was gentle. "How you doing, young lady? You okay?"

"I'm not sure."

"Were you here alone when you found her?"

"Yes. A hospice worker was supposed to be here. He agreed to stay while I went for a walk. But when I came back, he was gone."

Coroner Davis heard this as he came outside. "The hospice worker just left?"

"Apparently so. I went inside and found Gamma Rose not breathing." I tried and failed to keep my voice from cracking. "Her skin felt cold."

The men looked solemnly at their feet. "I'll need to ask you some questions for the death certificate," the coroner said. "Shall we sit in the kitchen? Or we can use my car, if you'd rather not go inside."

"The kitchen is fine. Will there be an autopsy?" My throat constricted at the thought of a Y incision in Gamma's fragile chest.

"It's not necessary since she was under hospice care. The death was expected and it appears to be natural causes."

The sheriff's radio sputtered from his pickup and he excused himself to answer. I led Ben into the kitchen and we sat at the table. I should have offered him something to drink, but I just stared at the scarred tabletop where Gamma and my mother and I once played cards. Gamma Rose had cackled with every hand she won.

I scooted the World Wildlife tote bag out of the way and Davis took a notepad from his bag. "Are you her next of kin?"

"As far as I know. She had a daughter, my grandmother, who disappeared years ago. I don't know if she's still living."

He asked me Gamma Rose's age, birthplace, and maiden name. I didn't know any of those things, and my eyes began to water. I was the world's worst great-granddaughter.

"Have you chosen a funeral home?" he asked.

"No. I'm not familiar with the area. Can you recommend one?"

"We're not allowed to recommend. But," he dug in his satchel and handed me a paper, "here's a list of all the licensed companies in the county. Her hospice might help you choose. We'll transport her to the coroner's office today. When you've decided on a funeral company, let me know and I'll release the body to them." He gave me his card.

While he used the land line to request an ambulance, I found a tissue and blew my nose. He wrote down Gamma's phone number and my cell, then we went outdoors again.

Sheriff Donovan was leaning against the front of his pickup. Mr. Davis spoke with him and I resumed my post on the front step to wait for the ambulance. My head buzzed and fatigue pulled at my shoulders.

The sheriff took a rag from his truck and dried off the chairs where Gamma and I would never again sit to watch nighttime gather in the woods. I had neglected to bring the chairs in out of the rain. The men sat respectfully silent for a while, then made quiet conversation. I wasn't listening. I thought about the arrangements I needed to make, and about Gamma's will that left the fenced acres behind the house to Zabella. And about Pesha.

"Sheriff Donovan," I blurted. "There's something I forgot to tell you."

Their faces turned toward me.

"When I was hiking on the mountain behind the house, I saw human bones in a deep fissure in the rocks."

The sheriff frowned. "Human? Are you sure?"

"Almost positive. There was a skull."

"Holy Roller," he muttered.

"I'm concerned they might belong to my grandmother. Gamma Rose's daughter who disappeared." My voice sounded hoarse. "And somebody took a shot at me while I was up there. I'm not sure whether it was a warning or they meant to kill me."

Sheriff Donovan's face darkened. He stood and gazed up the mountain slope, his eyes squinted and grim against the light. "Can you find the place again?"

"I'm sure I can. I ran back here intending to call you when I found Gamma Rose."

He nodded, still scanning the hillside. "I'll get together a recovery team, but we'll need you to show us the scene." He paused and looked at me. "I know you have to make arrangements and you're mourning your great-grandmother. But I'd like to recover the bones as soon as possible."

"So would I. And I want a DNA test."

"We can try. Sometimes DNA's hard to get if the bones are really old. Do you have a sample of your grandmother's DNA for comparison?"

"No, I'm afraid not. But if you take mine, we could learn if I was related, correct?"

"It's possible."

"The funeral won't be for a few days. Could we do it day after tomorrow?"

He nodded. "I'll try to get my team rounded up by then."

A boxy white vehicle lurched toward us up the driveway and the sheriff and coroner went to meet the driver. I couldn't watch them remove Gamma's body so I walked over to the chicken pen. Penny and Midnight queried me with subdued voices as if asking about their elderly keeper. I'd have to find a good home for these two. They were Gamma Rose's pets.

The clatter of wheels drew my eyes to the gurney exiting the house, whether I wanted to see it or not. A zippered bag lay on the cart with a heartbreakingly small form inside. My gut twisted. They loaded her into the ambulance, slammed the doors, and the vehicle rolled away.

Go slow, I begged. Don't toss her around on that bumpy road.

The coroner followed the ambulance in his type-cast black car. Sheriff Donovan stood with me, hat in his hands.

"Hate to leave you alone out here," he said. "Would you like to stay the night with my wife and me in town? She wouldn't mind, I promise."

I had to smile. Folks in Arkansas were just like Okies. "Thank you, sheriff. That's very kind, but I'll be okay. I need to make some phone calls and gather my thoughts."

He nodded. "Do you have any kind of weapon? For self-protection." When my eyebrows raised he added, "It pays to be careful."

He was thinking of the rifle shot, which I'd already forgotten. "There's a shotgun in her closet."

"Load it and keep it handy, just in case." He took a business card from his chest pocket. "My home number's on there. Call me if you need anything, no matter what time it is. I mean that."

From the look in his eyes, I knew he did. "Thanks. I'll stop by your office when I'm in Madison tomorrow."

"You do that. Take care then." He climbed into the gold truck and rumbled away.

Silence settled around me. In the woods, leaves dripped rainwater on the underbrush. All the activity at the house had hushed the birds and squirrels. The stillness seemed heavier knowing Gamma wasn't here. I was actually glad for the living presence of Penny and Midnight. They milled about inside their fence, pecking at hapless insects. Then a mockingbird resumed its song, and from the woods came the hammering of a pileated woodpecker. The sun disappeared behind the mountains. Shadows fell across me, though it wouldn't be dark for another hour or so. I heaved a sigh and went into the house.

A rolled mound of bedding sat in the corner of Gamma Rose's bedroom. Ben Davis had removed the sheets and mattress protector—a job Jake should have done as a hospice employee. I picked up the mound and took it outdoors to the burn barrel where Gamma disposed of her trash. I struck three matches and dropped them into the barrel one by one. When the sheets caught fire, I walked back to the house.

The tote bag with the items from the bank still lay on the kitchen table. I didn't get to show the pictures to Gamma Rose, but I was certain they were of Pesha. If the bones on the mountain proved to be hers, maybe science could determine her age when she died. So far, Gamma Rose's longevity was my single hope for a future.

If Pesha's husband did bring her back home, why would Gamma Rose say she'd sent her away? And why hadn't Pesha reclaimed her baby?

In the silent house, the kitchen phone trilled. For a moment I couldn't breathe, my heartbeat painful inside my ribs. Who would call here? The sheriff would still be on the road.

Maybe it was Jake. I ran to the phone and snatched the receiver on the fourth ring. "Hello?"

"Chantalene, it's Drew."

I sank into a kitchen chair. "Holy shit, I'm glad to hear from you."

"Really? That's flattering. I think." I could hear him smiling. "How are things going with your great-grandmother?"

"Give me a second to catch my breath." I inhaled deeply and then exhaled waiting for my heartbeat to stabilize while I decided where to start.

"Are you okay?" he said. "What's going on?"

I told him everything, starting with Gamma Rose's death, backtracking to my hike on the mountain and the discovery of the bones. I mentioned the shot fired over my head as an afterthought.

His voice tensed. "You're in danger there?"

"I don't think so," I said. "Maybe. But the local law is a good guy, and we're going to retrieve the bones as soon as we can. I'll need to arrange a funeral for Gamma Rose. There's so much to do...."

I was out of breath again and stopped talking. There was silence on the line.

Finally he said, "I was going to ask when you'd be back in Oklahoma, but obviously you can't know that. What can I do to help?"

His offer made my nose burn. "Nothing I can think of. But I appreciate it. Tomorrow I have to choose a funeral home and meet with them. I want to visit one of Gamma Rose's old friends who came to see her while I was here. Then there's the settling of her estate, which will likely require an attorney."

"I'm an attorney."

"Of course. But you're also in New York. An attorney here in Madison drew up her will, so I'm hoping he's still around." I sighed. "I really want to see you, though."

"Say the word and I'll be there."

I smiled, but was close to sobbing. This was the man I remembered and had missed so much. "That means the world to me. But it's such an expensive flight, and then a long drive. I'm kind of in a fog right now. Let me call you tomorrow."

"Okay." He paused. "If it helps, just remember I love you."

My mouth opened but no sound came out and he signed off.

He still loved me. There was no question that I still loved him. Somehow I would have to tell him I was a poor risk for a wife, that it was likely I wouldn't live long enough to raise children. But I simply couldn't do that right now.

In the over-stuffed living room, I flopped on the couch wishing for a strong shot of bourbon or at least a glass of wine. With no such thing available, I straightened my spine and decided to look at Gamma's will again. Maybe there was a phone number for the attorney she'd used.

Did Zabella know she would inherit the twenty acres? I wanted to question her about Pesha, and about who might have taken a pot shot at me up on the mountain. I bet that old woman owned a rifle and knew how to shoot. I felt certain she had answers to a lot of things if I could get her to talk. Maybe the impending DNA test would loosen her mole-less tongue.

I dumped the contents of the tote bag on the kitchen table. The bulky abstract fell out, and the brown envelope with the photographs. But nothing else. I shook the bag and peered inside.

It was empty. Where was the will?

I searched the floor under the table, the kitchen countertops, even the living room though I knew I hadn't taken it in there. The attorney's envelope was nowhere to be found.

I stood there, disbelieving. Gamma Rose's will was gone.

TEN

I WAS CERTAIN the coroner or sheriff hadn't taken Gamma's will. The only other person who'd been here was Jake.

What the hell?

I liked and trusted Jake. He was a dog person! Part of my brain thought that if I could only talk to him, he'd have a reasonable explanation. Another part told me to stop defending him. He had abandoned his patient and stolen her will.

I tried his cell number again. Still no answer. Finally it occurred to me to call the main number for the hospice.

The woman who answered had a voice made for sorrow. "I'm so sorry," she said when I asked for Jake. "He's out on a home visit this afternoon. Have you tried his cell?"

"Yes. He was supposed to be here with my great-grandmother. But while I was out, he deserted her."

"Oh, my! That's not like him at all. Shall I send out a different nurse?"

"It's a bit late for that. My great-grandmother has died."

While she was oh-dearing, I had another thought. "I'd like to speak with Doctor Bonaparte. Please ask him to call me as soon as possible. And if Jake shows up, I'd really like to talk to him."

It was evening now and nobody called back.

I knew only enough about funerals to realize I had to choose the clothes for Gamma Rose to be buried in. She'd left home in a nightgown, and that just wouldn't do.

Standing in the open door of her tiny closet, I inhaled the scents of sachet and dust and felt my nose prickle. Only four loose cotton dresses hung from the wooden rod. I chose a blue one that showed the least wear. The resplendent Gypsy shawl also went into the bag. She definitely should wear that to meet her maker.

Unable to sleep that night, I paced the rooms and finally stretched out on the couch. There were strange noises I hadn't noticed before. Something crashing through brush in the woods. A ticking noise from the kitchen. And a deep silence from Gamma Rose's bedroom. It was all I could do not to call Drew at one a.m. just to hear a sympathetic voice.

Instead I opted for comfort food. I craved ice cream but would have to settle for Honey Nut Cheerios. The cereal box wasn't in the cabinet. Had I eaten it all? I didn't think so. I couldn't find the granola bars, either. What the heck? Had Jake helped himself to a snack for the road?

I gave up and curled up like a squirrel on the sofa.

Daylight came at last. I fed the chickens, took a quick bath, and dressed for my chores in Madison with dread in my stomach. In Gamma's stained mirror, my eyes looked like the morning after a binge. Just before I walked out the door, the phone rang.

Dr. Bonaparte was returning my call. I told him what had happened.

"Really sorry for you. Even when it's expected, a loss like this is hard."

"Thank you. Have you heard anything from Jake?"

"I haven't checked in at the hospice facility yet this morning. His behavior worries me because he's been a dependable worker for us."

"I thought so too. He was good with my great-grandmother, but leaving her unattended is inexcusable." I didn't accuse Jake of stealing the will. Not yet.

"I agree," he said.

"I was just leaving for Madison to locate a funeral service. Do you have a recommendation?"

"When my mother died, we used Matthews Funeral Home," he said. "It's family owned and the staff was professional and kind. It's a block south of the hospital."

"That's good to know. Thank you."

I locked the house and drove toward town, my stomach twisting like the narrow roads. How did one plan a fitting funeral for an nonagenarian Gypsy woman with a prophetic mole on her tongue? What had become of Jake? How soon could I go back to my quiet farm in Oklahoma?

The Matthews Funeral Home was conveniently located just past the hospice facility in a buff brick building with a wide porte-cochere on one side. I was met in the reception area by Mr. Matthews himself, who spoke through a voice amplifier held to an opening in his neck, possibly the result of throat cancer. He had a slight build, kind brown eyes, and a striped suit just a tad too large. He ushered me into his tastefully subdued office.

We planned a simple service in their chapel three days later. If the old Romanies were insulted by a gadže funeral, let them stay home. I would lay my great-grandmother to rest with dignity even if I was the only mourner.

"I've found no record of a burial plot," I told Mr. Matthews. "Is there a cemetery close?"

His brow creased. "There is, and I believe she has family buried in the old section, where most of the Gypsies go."

Small towns. The undertaker would know pretty much everybody in the cemetery.

"I remember now," I said. "Her husband Yoors was buried there. She said she wanted to be next to him."

"That sounds right. I'll check on it for you."

I gave Mr. Matthews the grocery bag with Gamma Rose's burial clothes. After the disheartening task of choosing a casket, I phoned the coroner and gave permission to release Gamma's body to Mr. Matthews's establishment.

I sat in my car to phone Sheriff Donovan.

"Morning, sheriff, it's Chantalene. I'm in Madison and wondered if I could stop by your office."

"Please do," he said. "I've contacted the recovery team."

The main drag of Madison was four blocks bordered by angled parking with many of the spaces empty. At the end sat a brick building where a small sign staked out the county sheriff's office. An adjacent grassy area held huge trees and a decaying band shell. Today it was vacant and peaceful with yellow and brown leaves littering the ground.

I parked and went inside. When I found the correct door, a young woman in uniform ushered me to see Sheriff Donovan. He stood when I entered his office, motioned me to a chair, then fixed me with a serious gaze. "How are you doing this morning?"

"Better than yesterday," I said. "Are your people coming out to the house tomorrow?"

"About ten a.m., if that's okay. Weather's supposed to be clear. The team will bring ropes and a stretcher and anything else they need."

"I'm not sure a stretcher will fit in that fissure. A basket of some kind might work better. The bones are"—I searched for a suitable word—"not all together."

He nodded. "We'll bring that, too. But we want to keep the skeleton intact as much as possible. Might tell us something about the manner of death."

I did not confess my excitement for the grisly task. Those bones might explain the disappearance of Pesha and I was keen to know whatever they might tell us.

The sheriff swabbed the inside of my cheeks for DNA, and I asked one more question.

"Can you give me directions to the home of Zabella Mallosh? She came to visit Gamma Rose."

The sheriff nodded. "I think she lives close to your great-grandmother's place. Let me check." He pulled up an app on his desktop computer and scratched out a map on paper. "Some of the roads out that way don't have names."

It turned out Zabella lived less than half a mile from Gamma's place, though you couldn't see the house for the trees. That explained why she had walked the night she came to see Gamma Rose. Maybe the older Romani all lived close together out in the country. I thanked the sheriff and left with his diagram in hand.

Next I stopped at the bank to see Mr. Barrington. When I tapped on the window of his glass-walled office, he quickly closed the laptop on his desk. Spider solitaire? I wondered. Or maybe online poker.

"Miss Morrell!" he called. "Come in. Nice to see you again."

An embroidered sampler that hung behind his desk advised Do Unto Others. I wondered exactly what the banker did unto others. Unlike Gamma Rose, I was skeptical of gadže bankers.

"Do you have a moment?" I asked.

"Of course." He gestured toward the visitor's chair and I sat. "I came to notify you that my great-grandmother has died. I may need your help with a few things."

Mr. Barrington looked somber. "I'm sorry for your loss."

"Thank you. She left me in charge of her affairs, so at some point I'll need access to her accounts for funeral expenses."

"I understand. Do you have a document naming you as executor of her estate?"

Estate seemed like a pretty big word for Gamma Rose's belongings. "That's the thing. There was a will in her safe deposit box, but it has disappeared."

His eyebrows lifted. "You lost it?"

"I don't see how. It was right on the kitchen table, but now it's gone. I'm hoping the attorney who drew it up might have saved an electronic copy, but I can't remember his name."

"Ah, well. There are three attorneys practicing in town. I expect it's either Robert Atwood, Sam Gillingham, or Dell Sampson."

"Sampson. That's it." Once he'd said it, I could picture the name on the envelope that held Gamma's will. "If he has the will, I'll bring you a copy."

"Perfect. Anything else I can do?"

Maybe he was anxious to get back to his computer game. "Not at the moment, thank you." He stood again as I left his office.

On the sidewalk outside the bank, where my cell actually had enough reception, I Googled Dell Sampson attorney. Up popped his office address and a phone number. I pushed the call button.

Mr. Sampson's assistant was sorry, but Dell was not in at the moment. I told her what I needed.

"I can check the files for a copy of Mrs. Tsura's will, but I can't give it to you without Dell's okay. He'll want to make sure you are next of kin."

"I understand. Please ask Mister Sampson to call me."

She promised she would. I hung up, then on impulse tried Jake's cell number. No answer.

By now it was noon, so I cruised down to the Sonic Drive-In and ordered a grilled cheese and root-beer float. I ate in the car and prepared myself for a visit to Zabella. I wasn't sure she'd be happy to see me, but notifying her of Gamma Rose's death in person seemed like the right thing to do. I also hoped she could answer some of my questions. It might be tricky getting her to talk. I was half gadžu, after all.

I laid my head back on the seat and thought of my feisty great-grandmother. A weary sadness washed over me, regret for our lack of time together. It was one of those things I couldn't change and would have to accept. I finished my root beer with a heartfelt slurp and affixed the sheriff's map to the dashboard with a sticker from the sandwich wrapper.

Zabella's place was buried in the woods, even harder to find than Gamma Rose's. The map was close but not perfect. I passed the driveway going both directions, the second time backing up until I spied a two-track path boring into thick brush. If the trees hadn't already shed some of their leaves, I might never have found it. The obscurity felt intentional.

The house was made of logs turned gray with age. It looked larger than Gamma's, and less friendly. On one side, an addition that didn't match the house was covered with clapboard that had once been painted orange with blue trim. Zabella was nothing if not colorful. Perhaps she had a big family once, but I was guessing she now lived alone. She was younger than Gamma Rose, but not by much. Maybe mid-eighties.

I parked a respectful distance from the house in an unfenced dooryard. The scraggly patch of grass surrounding the house was littered with old tires and odd scraps of metal. A child's wooden chair lay on its side, only a few flecks of red paint remaining. Three skinny hounds arose to bark at me.

As soon as I stepped out of the vehicle, Zabella appeared at the front entrance, her face as stony as Mt. Rushmore. She wore a long skirt in a cobalt blue print and an orange dikla over her hair. I began to see a pattern here.

I approached. "I came to tell you that Gamma Rose died yesterday."

The old Gypsy nodded, her expression unchanged. "I heard. Come in. I will make tea." Without waiting for an answer, she turned and disappeared into the shadowy interior.

The invitation surprised me, and my hopes of gaining information from her rose. I stepped through the door and paused, unsure what to do. The house was cool inside and dark as a cave. From the kitchen I heard the sound of a kettle being put on to heat. After a long moment, she called, "Close the door. Were you born in a stable?"

"I was born in the backyard on a straw bed, which my mother burned afterward. At least that's what I was told." I still didn't move except to shut the door.

Zabella returned carrying a tray. "The Romani way. I'm surprised LaVita would follow the customs." Though she didn't smile, she looked satisfied by this bit of knowledge. "Sit down."

It was more a command than an invitation. I sat and she returned to the kitchen.

Her living room was larger than Gamma's and almost as crowded. The sofa and chairs bloomed with magenta roses on a background that might have once been navy blue or dark purple. They faced a large modern television. In contrast to the front lawn, the room looked freshly scrubbed.

Framed Western movie posters, yellowed but dust free, decorated the walls. John Wayne, Gary Cooper, Clint Eastwood. Beneath the scent of Pine Sol curled a bouquet like incense or skunkweed. It was not a pleasant mixture.

In a moment she returned holding a cast-iron teakettle with two oven mitts and poured steaming water into a china pot on the tray. The aroma of tea was welcome and pure. She returned the kettle to the stove and joined me, sitting in a chair across from the sofa, the tray between us on a coffee table. "Sugar or milk?" she asked.

"No, thanks."

She spooned three sugars into her own cup and added a splash of milk before pouring dark tea for us both. The cups were different patterns, and I knew mine was set aside for visitors.

Zabella settled back in her chair with a grunt, steadying her cup in two gnarled hands. "I hope she went peacefully."

"She did, yes."

The old woman nodded. "We had our differences, but I respected your great-grandmother. We were friends for many years."

"Thank you. I respected her, too." I sipped my tea and shifted in my seat. The flavor was exotic, definitely not Earl Grey. "Did you know that she left the twenty acres behind her house to you?"

Her eyebrows raised a fraction. She nodded, but said nothing.

"I assume it was to protect the identity of the bones I found up there. The ones you were willing to shoot me to keep secret."

This was speculation, but she didn't deny it. Her eyes narrowed for only a second, then she gazed impassively into her tea.

"If I'd meant to kill you, you would be dead."

This admission sent a flash of heat through me, and suddenly I wondered about the tea I was drinking. I put down my cup.

"I need to know what happened to my grandmother Pesha. It's a matter of concern about my medical history. Are those her bones?"

She shrugged. "Who knows?"

I watched her a moment without speaking, and she watched me back.

"Who is Ian? Gamma Rose asked you about him."

Her eyes turned even darker, and her layered chin lifted. "Ian was my son. The foolish boy Pesha ran away with." Her mouth twisted. "They were in love."

"You told Gamma Rose that Ian had died."

"This is what I heard. My son was lost to me after he ran away."

I heard grief in her voice. "You loved him very much," I said.

"Of course. I had three daughters, but only one son. He was a good boy, devoted and artistic. I would have done anything for him."

Anything? Did that include murder?

"I'm sorry about your son. Could you please tell me about Pesha? I have no other relatives left."

Zabella sighed and hoisted her bulk from the soft chair. She crossed to a cupboard near a blackened fireplace and extracted a bottle. When she uncapped it, the aroma of rum drifted to me, unmistakable. She poured a generous splash into her teacup and offered the bottle to me. I shook my head. She set it on the table and sank again into her chair.

"Pesha was a beautiful child, but headstrong. She spent every minute with her father and his horses, and she inherited his gift for handling them. She worshipped Yoors, and his death was horrible for her."

"Yes. Gamma Rose told me this much."

"Did she tell you Pesha was with him that day? She saw the snake and yelled to her father, but it was too late. The snake struck at the horse's leg. It reared and fell backward onto Yoors."

I cringed to think of a young girl seeing her much-loved father die.

Zabella's voice scraped. "Pesha got the hoe and killed that snake. Chopped it into bloody pieces in the dirt. Then she ran to the barn and got Yoors's shotgun. When Gamma Rose came out of the house and found them, Pesha was standing over the horse with the gun. It's leg was broken. She shot the horse in the head before Gamma Rose could grab her up and carry her away."

My throat closed. I imagined the fury that drove Pesha to kill the things that had killed her father. "My god," I whispered. "That's horrible."

Zabella nodded. "After that, Gamma Rose spoiled the girl, trying to make her happy. But she was uncontrollable. Her Uncle Luca tried to help, but she would do the opposite of whatever he said.

"When she was twelve, Luca talked to Gamma Rose about finding her a husband. This was his duty as an uncle, but Pesha rejected traditions. She measured every man against her father and none met the standard. None except Ian. He was smitten with her, but we were poor and had no money for a daro."

I kept quiet and pretended to sip my tea, but my heart raced. This was a part of the story Gamma Rose wouldn't tell me. Maybe it was too painful for her.

Zabella finished her rum tea and leaned back in her chair. "Gamma Rose wanted Pesha to have a wealthy husband who could provide well for them both. This was only right because she was a widow. I wanted the same thing for my daughters. When Pesha was fourteen, Luca brought a man around and introduced them. Tobar Kaldera. Pesha was beautiful, tall and strong, and the man was pleased. He said she could give him many handsome children. He made a deal with Uncle Luca to pay a bride price of five thousand dollars. In those days, this was a huge amount of money. Luca said Gamma Rose could invest it and be financially secure."

I tried to understand my great-grandmother's difficult decision. I had no right to judge her. I hadn't lived in her society, where girls' long skirts must never pass over any part of a man's body, and women were considered unclean during their menses. Daughters were married for expediency, not love, and a man who couldn't offer a good bride price had no right to propose.

I held my breath, hoping Zabella would continue, and she did.

"Tobar was in his thirties—an old man to Pesha, and therefore repulsive. He was a bachelor and Pesha thought something must be wrong with a man that age who'd never married." Zabella stifled a smirk. "Probably she was right. But he was wealthy and a good catch. Pesha wailed and cried, so Gamma Rose agreed to wait until she was sixteen. Maybe by then she would come to her senses, or have a better offer. If not, she would have to marry him anyway."

"What about Ian?"

"Pesha and Ian sneaked around to be together. But he had asthma that made physical work impossible, and Gamma Rose considered him weak. At sixteen Pesha was married to Tobar, under threat of bolime. Exile from her kumpania." Her forehead wrinkled into a frown. "Ian was so distraught I worried he might harm himself. He refused to pursue other girls."

I pictured the two young lovers like Romeo and Juliet, locked in a forbidden love. We are never more passionate about love or injustice than when we are teenagers.

"It is true that in her mother-in-law's house," Zabella said, "Pesha was worked like a slave and not treated with respect. Tobar forced himself on her relentlessly and beat her if she resisted. Within three months she was pregnant. She came crying to Gamma Rose, saying she hated her husband and did not want to bear his children. Gamma told her the truth. Life wasn't easy, she should toughen up and accept it. When she had a baby of her own, the in-laws would treat her better.

"And did they?"

"Her mother-in-law did. But Pesha delivered a baby girl. Your mother. Tobar had wanted a son."

"Did everyone in the kumpania know how her husband treated her?"

Zabella added rum to her cup and didn't bother with more tea. I was happy with that because it kept her talking.

"Your great-grandmother and I were close friends before our children ran away. We kept each other's secrets. But Tobar's behavior was a secret to no one."

"How did Ian and Pesha get back together?"

"They kept in touch, even though it was forbidden." Zabella's voice took on a tinge of bitterness. "When her baby was weaned from the breast, Pesha convinced Ian to help her escape from her husband. She left the baby with Gamma Rose and they ran away to Missouri where she hoped to get a divorce."

I remembered what Gamma had told me and leaned forward. "I know Tobar went after her. What happened then?"

A veil of impenetrability settled over her face. She blinked as if she had talked too much. "I know only that my son was lost forever."

She stood without warning. "You should go now. I am sorry for your loss."

Leaving our teacups on the table, she walked through a curtained doorway and left me sitting in unfinished silence.

I waited ten minutes to see if she would return, then let myself out.

ELEVEN

AT MID-MORNING, Sheriff Donovan's pickup rolled up to Gamma's house, followed by a white SUV. I met them in the yard.

Steve and Audrey Mason, the man-and-wife recovery team, were slim and athletic-looking, a handsome couple. The sheriff introduced us. With a petite build and pixie haircut, Audrey didn't look big enough to recover anybody, but her body language told me not to underestimate her.

The Masons wore army-style fatigues and hard hats, their pants tucked into hiking boots. From the back of their SUV they unpacked a jumble of ropes, spikes, netting, and safety belts. They loaded up like pack animals and Steve gave Sheriff Donovan a half salute.

"Ready to roll."

The sheriff looked to me. I led them behind the cabin to the gate in the chain-link fence. With all their gear, the team couldn't squeeze through the small opening I had made. Audrey dispatched undergrowth and maple branches with a machete. Steve pried the gate back on its hinges and we were in.

We hiked upward in single file, following the left fence line where I'd gone before. The day was cool but sunny. Before long I was sweating, and I didn't have on heavy clothes and a bunch of gear like my companions. If the others were steaming, they didn't complain.

When I spotted the back fence through the trees ahead of us, I turned right on a parallel path. We crossed the small stream and then the larger one. I kept plodding, imagining that my companions wondered what was taking so long. The trek seemed farther than it had before, but finally the limestone crags rose ahead of us above the trees.

I stopped and pointed. "Up there."

My heartbeat was loud in my ears as I trudged forward. We stopped at the base of the steep formation and the team gazed upward, assessing the climb.

"Piece of cake," Audrey said. For them, it probably was.

Steve took the lead and found an easier path than I had previously ascended. We climbed over boulders and gaps in the rocks. I worried that the bones would be gone and I'd be revealed as bat-crazy. But when we finally stood on the top and peered into the crevasse, bone-white remains glowed in the shadowy depths.

"All right," Steve said. "We'll get set up. You were right about the stretcher— that's not going to fit. We'll use the canvas bag for recovery."

The sheriff surveyed his surroundings. "This is where you were standing when you heard the rifle shot?"

"Yes. If the shooter was actually aiming at me, I'd have been hard to miss."

"Maybe. Could you tell where the shot came from?"

I pointed toward the east. "Somewhere in that direction."

He shook his head. "We'd never find a casing in this brush, even if he left one."

"Or she." But I didn't tell him what Zabella had said. Maybe another time. I was more interested in identifying the fragmented skeleton.

Steve and Audrey drove spikes to anchor their ropes and Steve strapped on a harness. There was no need—or room—for both of them to go down and, being a man, Steve preempted her. Audrey was in charge of managing the ropes to make sure they held. The chasm was narrow, with just enough room for a body to fall between the vertical walls. My every orifice tightened as Steve lowered himself over the edge.

They worked methodically, not hurrying, making safety a priority. I leaned over to watch his descent and my balance wavered. I backed up a few steps, tense as a mouse in a cattery. Was that my grandmother down there, or some other hapless soul? I wondered if we'd ever know how it happened.

"I need more light," Steve called up.

The sheriff moved to the edge and aimed a powerful flashlight into the depths of the fissure. When Steve was in position, Audrey lowered the canvas bag and plastic gloves. They talked back and forth, adjusting the rope that held his harness as he moved sideways to collect the bones that had separated from the others.

"I've got the skull," Steve called. "Most of it, anyway."

I turned away, my stomach queasy, and gazed over the treetops toward the place where the streams converged. In the dense brush, an unexpected movement caught my eye. I waited a moment and saw a doe and fawn approach the stream from the far side. A welcome sign of life that made me smile.

How did they get in here? The fence was too tall for even deer to leap, and it had been here for decades. I didn't think a population of deer could have existed inside since that time. The only other explanation was an opening somewhere in the fence.

I scanned the trees where the deer had appeared, squinting against the light. I had explored three boundaries of the property, but not the side where the sun came up. The direction the rifle shot had come from.

I turned to Sheriff Donovan. "If there's nothing I can do to help, I'll meet you back at the house. Can you find your way down?"

"No problem," he said, peering into the slash where his flashlight beam disappeared. "Even if I couldn't, Steve and Audrey are like radar dogs."

I couldn't quite picture a radar dog, but I didn't doubt the Masons.

My sneakers created an avalanche of pebbles on my slow descent. I wished for hiking boots like Audrey's. Once at the bottom, I bushwhacked my way eastward, arriving at the boundary sooner than I expected. I could see that the fence was intact all the way uphill, so I moved downline looking for a breach. About half way, I found it. The wires had been cut from the bottom up and curled back from their post. The triangular opening was large enough for a deer—or person—to walk through. So I did.

Ducking my head, I stepped into tall grass on the other side. There were fewer trees here, though the land was still wild. I tramped a few paces and climbed onto a fallen tree trunk to see what I could see. Maybe two hundred feet below, the roofline of an asymmetrical house showed through the brush. The cracked shingles were littered with sticks and moss, and a driveway angled off toward the main road.

I recognized the odd architecture. Zabella's house. She lived right next door to Gamma Rose's land, and she—or someone—had created easy access.

Her hounds set up a racket near the house, barking in my direction. A built-in warning system. I jumped off the log and darted back through the opening, then stood a moment gazing through the fence. I had the sense that I'd learned something important but didn't understand what it meant.

The recovery team would be finishing up, so I started back to the house. Rushing water was my landmark. I tramped toward the sound, stepping over thorny vines and rabbit trails. Ahead, a light-colored mass lay amidst the brush. I squinted through the trees. Perhaps I'd come upon on the deer. But my inelegant plodding would have scared them away, and the object on the ground didn't move. I clapped my hands. Still no movement. Probably trash, blown here by the wind.

But as I came closer, stepping slowly, the tan color became a shirt with the form of a person inside. God, no.

Jake lay on his side at the base of a tree, as if he'd toppled over there. I dropped to my knees beside him. A brownish-red stain that could only be blood spread over one leg of his pants.

I shook his shoulder. "Jake! Jake, can you hear me?"

He didn't move. I searched his neck for a pulse, but mine was beating so hard I couldn't tell if the throbbing was my heart or his. Very gently, I rolled him on his back and pressed my ear to his chest.

A heartbeat. Thank god.

The Masons had a stretcher. I charged upstream until the rocky cliff appeared to my left and voices drifted down to me. I planted my feet and screamed upward.

"Sheriff Donovan! Sheriff Donovan, can you hear me?" A few beats of silence, then I heard the sheriff's voice.

"I hear you," he yelled. "What's wrong?"

"I've found a wounded man down here. Bring the stretcher!"

"Holy Roller! We're finished here. Stay where you are so we can find you."

"THAT'S A BULLET wound," the sheriff said after splitting the leg of Jake's jeans with his pocket knife.

"He's lost a lot of blood and he's dehydrated," Audrey said. "We need to get him to a hospital fast."

Team Mason handled Jake's limp body with careful efficiency. Steve and the sheriff carried the stretcher. Audrey and I lugged the gear and walked ahead, hacking a path for the men to follow through. When we finally reached the vehicles in the dooryard, everyone except Jake was breathing heavily.

"We can get him to the hospital in our car faster than waiting on an ambulance," Steve said. He flattened the back seat of their SUV and they loaded Jake into the back. Audrey crawled in to keep him steady and Steve zoomed away.

"If he was up there the other day when that shot was fired, maybe that's what hit him," I said.

"It's possible," the sheriff said. "You didn't hear a second shot?"

"No."

Again, I hesitated to name Zabella as the shooter. Her confession was vague, and I wanted information from her that I'd never get if I accused her and she was arrested.

He loaded the equipment and bagged bones into the cab of his truck and followed the Masons. I stood alone in the driveway, my heartbeat hammering.

I had not thought that Jake might be part of my family mystery until Gamma's will went missing. Now I reconsidered. People usually didn't get involved in others' affairs unless they wanted something. I couldn't figure out Jake's motive. Much as I wanted to question him, he wouldn't be talking for a while, assuming he survived.

Suddenly I thought of Jake's dog, T-Bone. If Jake had been on the mountain since Gamma's death, had the dog not been fed for two days? I didn't know where he lived, but someone at the hospice facility surely would. I went inside to call them.

I told the nurse who answered the phone that Jake was in the hospital. She wasn't allowed to give out Jake's address but promised they would send someone to his house to take care of the dog. She sounded concerned enough that I believed her.

———————————

THE HOUSE WAS eerily quiet. I made a cucumber and cheese sandwich and sat at the kitchen table with pen and yellow notepad. Despite my rattled mind after finding Jake, tomorrow was Gamma Rose's funeral and I needed to write her eulogy.

I didn't know her well until the past week, but the generic pastor recruited by the funeral director hadn't known her at all. Someone should testify about the exceptional woman she was. I intended to do so, even if nobody was there to hear.

My hand was jittery holding the pen. Where to start? I didn't know where Gamma Rose was born, or even exactly when. Her parents were nameless to me. So I began with the tale she'd told me when I was ten, about traveling with the Zingaro caravan all across the South before the clan finally settled in the Ozarks. As a child she danced to Gypsy music around campfires, helped water the horses from the rivers and streams where they camped.

I wrote about her arranged marriage to Yoors, how he was good to her and she came to respect him, maybe even love him. About her runaway daughter Pesha, and the granddaughter she had raised on her own, my mother. And how much my mother loved her.

Tears made dark yellow spots on the pages.

I described the mole on her tongue and her gift of foresight, the people who came to her for prophecy and advice. Who was I to doubt her gift, when I myself saw auras that other people couldn't? Hers was a long life and not an easy one. Gamma Rose hadn't considered her life hard, but lucky. I laid my head on my folded arms and mourned.

After a while I made tea and stood at the front window looking out. I watched twilight gather in the woods, and I said goodbye to my redoubtable great-grandmother.

TWELVE

PENNY AND MIDNIGHT circled me cautiously, bobbing their feathered necks as I scattered feed in the yard the next morning. The sun hadn't quite cleared the treetops and yellow light sparkled through the thinning leaves. Other than the loamy scent of chicken kibbles, the air smelled full of oxygen.

The hens were almost, but not quite, okay with my feeding them instead of Gamma Rose. She had been their loyal friend. "You ladies want to go to her funeral?" I asked. "I could use the company."

Getting no response from the little cluckers, I collected two eggs and went inside to get dressed.

It was a lonely drive to Madison. I arrived early and Mr. Matthews escorted me to a small chapel. Gamma Rose's closed casket sat at the front. I stopped at the back and took a shaky breath. It was a shock to see someone I loved sealed up like that.

The silver burial chest was wreathed in flowers. I had ordered the casket piece, but not the others. I turned to Mr. Matthews. "Where did all these flowers come from?"

He held his voice amplifier to the hole in his neck. "Your great-grandmother had many friends." He offered me a stack of tiny envelopes. "I thought you'd want to see the cards. With your permission, we'll leave the flowers on her grave after the service."

"Of course. Thank you."

"The large arrangement on the right, the red and white roses, didn't have a card. I called the florist and she said they were ordered anonymously."

"Really? Is that common?"

"No. Quite unusual." He gave a slight bow. "I'll leave you with your loved one now." He backed out of the room as if leaving royalty.

On each envelope someone had noted the color and kind of flowers so I could identify them. I walked to the front of the room and stood beside the arrangements, opening the cards one by one. White lilies from Gamma's banker. Carnations and daisies from the lawyer who'd drafted her will. And a bright orange bouquet from Zabella. Yikes.

A few cards were signed with several Romani names. The only name I recognized was Lucinda, the girl who had come to Gamma for advice on her fiancé. The last card—a beautiful arrangement of yellow spider mums and violet gladiolas—was from Drew. The internet is a magical thing.

Seeing his name wilted my knees and made my nose run. I touched the cool petals as if that could bring him closer.

The spray of roses Mr. Matthews had mentioned stood on an easel beside the casket. The hothouse buds were flawless and fragrance-free. In all that lavish greenery, maybe he'd simply overlooked the card. I pawed through the fronds but found nothing. Who would send such an elaborate remembrance and choose to remain anonymous? A secret admirer?

My brain frequency-hopped to the unidentified visitor who came to Gamma's house in the night. A connection seemed unlikely. I stuffed the cards into my purse.

Canned organ music seeped through the room. Over its soft strains I heard the tuneless chirp of a robin and the wind tapping a branch against the window. An invisible clock ticked, or maybe that was inside my head. I laid my palm on the cold casket and reminded myself to breathe.

"I'll miss you, Gamma Rose." My voice sounded eerie in the silence. "Even though I came late to the party, I feel like we connected. I loved your strength and your sense of humor. Even the mole on your tongue." I felt her smile at that, and I smiled, too.

A shadow appeared at my shoulder and I looked up to see Mr. Matthews with another man. He introduced the pastor but I didn't catch his name.

"It's ten o'clock. Shall we begin?" the director said.

I took a seat on the front row. The organ music cranked up a notch, then faded to silence as the pastor took the podium. Mr. Matthews and a woman I recognized as an employee, obviously recruited, sat on the front row across the aisle from me. No one else was there.

I really should have brought Penny and Midnight, I told Gamma Rose, and imagined her raspy laugh.

The pastor called for prayer. Beneath his words, I heard the back door whisper open and close. Maybe I wouldn't be the only voluntary mourner after all. When the prayer was finished, he read a short scripture aimed to give hope for a life beyond. I had declined any pastoral message or singing. There was a limit to how many trappings of a gadže funeral Gamma Rose would tolerate.

The pastor invited me to come forward and give the eulogy. I walked to the lectern gripping my handwritten pages. When I finally lifted my eyes, I saw that two people had entered and were seated apart in the back rows. Zabella wore a black dikla, her hand resting on the tiger-headed cane, her face like stone. I was glad that she'd come.

It took a moment to realize the other person was Drew.

My breath escaped in a rush and I grabbed the lectern with both hands. An inappropriate grin spread across my face and I said aloud, "Drew. You're here."

My words vibrated in the near-empty room. The woman employee turned her head to look, but Mr. Matthews and the pastor remained solemn, eyes to the front. Drew nodded and returned my smile.

I cleared my throat and unfolded the pages, smoothing them out on the lectern. I managed to read my tribute without choking up. When I'd finished, Drew gave me a subtle thumbs up.

I resumed my seat and the reverend offered a closing prayer. Nothing left but the burial.

Mr. Matthews and his helper rolled Gamma down the aisle toward a side door where the hearse was waiting. I followed, but stopped to hug Drew. His arms felt good around me, natural. I remembered his smell. All our history arose in a rush and I held on for a long time. Whatever crazy reason I'd had for giving this up, I regretted it deeply.

I nodded to Zabella, a thanks for coming. Drew and I held hands as we walked out.

The day was already surreal, but nothing prepared me for the sight that greeted me outdoors. An antique Gypsy wagon sat on the street, a stunning anachronism beside the late-model black hearse. The wagon was festooned with flowers and multi-colored ribbons that streamed from its roof in the autumn breeze. In the driver's seat sat a gray-haired Romani wearing blousy black pants and a brightly patterned shirt. He held a battered hat over his heart.

I wondered how many years the wagon had been in storage. The paint was barely faded. Had Zabella arranged this tribute to my great-grandmother?

Behind the wagon, two vintage Cadillacs idled, also beribboned. Half a dozen Gypsies in traditional garb waited on foot behind the cars. Behind them stood two pairs of shiny dark horses with flowers woven into their manes and tails. All were riderless, with bright blankets draped on their backs. Dark-eyed young men held the bridles of each horse.

Gamma Rose, are you seeing this? They are honoring you. My eyes filled and Drew squeezed my hand tighter. Though I'd always known of my Gypsy heritage, I hadn't felt a part of it. Growing up as a farm girl, I never thought about where I'd inherited my black hair and dark eyes. I knew nothing of Romani customs or language. My mother told me stories of the grandmother who'd raised her only when I begged. But seeing this cultural show of respect for Gamma Rose, I felt like one of them.

Four of the men came to lift Gamma's casket into the back of the hearse. Drew stepped forward to help but was waved away. When she was safely inside, chapel employees began loading the flowers.

Mr. Matthews opened the back passenger door of the family car, a black Lincoln, and motioned Drew and me inside. I turned to offer Zabella a ride, but she was already climbing into one of the Cadillacs.

The cemetery lay at the south edge of town, only a short distance away. Our caravan rolled down Main Street, ignoring red lights. The horses' hooves echoed on the pavement, and someone in the procession beat a drum slowly. A rainbow of ribbons arched in the wind. On the sidewalks, pedestrians stopped to stare. Men took off their hats.

I had stepped into a Quentin Tarantino movie, but without the blood.

At the cemetery, the hearse pulled close to an open grave and the caravan rolled to a stop on the gravel path. Romani men carried Gamma's casket and placed it on the heavy straps that would lower her into the earth. There were no chairs for mourners because we hadn't expected any. I stood at the head of the casket, Drew beside me, and everyone from the caravan gathered around.

The pastor edged through the ring of people to the graveside. "Lord, we commit into your hands the soul of Gamma Rose Tsura. May she be welcomed by Jesus and her husband Yoors." Then, as an afterthought, "Dust to dust, ashes to ashes."

He nodded to Mr. Matthews. The funeral director had extracted two long-stemmed roses from the anonymous arrangement, and he handed them to Drew and me. Then he stood back and folded his hands. A pause ensued, as if nobody knew what was supposed to happen next.

Finally, I cleared my throat and addressed the circle of faces. "Thank you for coming. It means a great deal to me, and I know Gamma Rose would be pleased." I laid the rose on the casket and stepped back. Drew did the same.

With no visible signal, Zabella separated from the circle. She placed her hand on the casket and said something in Romani that I didn't understand. The others mumbled assent. Then they fell in line behind her.

One by one they filed past. Some picked up a stone and threw it over their shoulders. Others tossed coins onto the casket. The sound was like hail on a metal roof. The ritual continued until all had passed by and walked back toward the caravan.

The last woman in the line stopped beside me. I recognized her as one of the old ones who had come to Gamma Rose's room at the hospice.

"I loved your great-grandmother," she said, her voice like sand. "I brought her groceries after she couldn't drive." She paused, nodding. "You must burn her possessions. Or sell them only to gadže. It is the old tradition, and she was an old Gypsy."

She lifted my hand and placed a smooth, round stone in my palm. I looked at it, and then into her eyes. With my right hand, I tossed the stone over my left shoulder. She nodded sharply and moved on.

The caravan left the cemetery, but I stayed until Gamma Rose was lowered into the ground and the flowers mounded on her grave.

Mr. Matthews drove Drew and me back to our cars. I thanked him and arranged to come by later to pay the bill.

Drew's rental was parked next to mine on the street outside the funeral home. "Can you come out to the house and stay awhile?" I asked.

"Of course. I took a week off work."

I wanted to hug him but restrained myself, for now. "I'm so glad. It means a lot to me that you came."

He smiled. "Are you kidding? I wouldn't have missed that parade for the world."

"Amazing, wasn't it? I had no idea." I dug car keys from my purse. "I do have to stop by the hospital on the way home. There's someone I need to check on. The hospital is straight up this street."

"I'll follow you." He stopped and met my eyes. "It's great to see you. Despite everything, you look terrific."

I laughed for the first time in days. "I doubt that seriously. But thanks for saying so."

We drove in tandem the few blocks to the hospital. I parked and went to his driver-side window. "Do you want to come with me?"

"Why don't I go pick us up some lunch while you're inside. I saw a fast food place on the way. All I've had since yesterday is airline coffee and pretzels."

I grinned. "By all means. No meat for me."

"How could I forget?" He smiled and drove away.

In the intensive care unit where Jake was a patient, I talked to the charge nurse.

"We're keeping him in ICU overnight," she said. "He was in surgery several hours to remove bone chips and re-set the femur. He'll be in a cast at least six weeks."

"Are you family?" she asked.

"No, a friend. As far as I know, he has no family here." I wasn't sure about this, but I wanted to persuade her. "Can I see him?"

"That's up to the officer posted by his room."

Sheriff Donovan was taking the gunshot wound more seriously than I'd expected. I checked in with the local cop on guard duty, who looked bored to distraction. He let me step into Jake's cubicle but kept an eye on me from the door.

Jake was sleeping soundly, his tanned face slack against the white sheets. Nobody looks good after surgery. A heart monitor beeped, and an IV trailed from his arm. His left leg was elevated slightly and encased in a fiberglass cast. I'd had one of those hip casts once, and they were no darned fun. I felt bad for him, but I still wanted to know why he took Gamma's will and was trespassing on her property.

I left the room and approached the nurse again. "Would you please call me when he's able to talk?"

I wrote my cell number and Gamma's land line on a scrap of paper, but her grudging assent didn't convince me she would call. So I asked for the direct phone number to the ICU and tapped it into my phone, intending to check back in the morning.

While I waited outside the entrance for Drew to return, I phoned Sheriff Donovan.

"I'm glad you called," he said. "A forensic anthropologist from the university took a look at those bones. They don't belong to your grandmother."

"How do you know?"

"Because this person was a man."

THIRTEEN

THE BONES BELONGED to a man, not Pesha. On the drive from the hospital to Gamma Rose's house, I tried to figure out what this meant. Who could they belong to? According to Zabella, both Ian and Tobar disappeared, as well as Pesha. Did one of those men end up on the mountain? Or were the bones completely unrelated to my grandmother's disappearance? I'd have to hope the DNA analysis would give us a clue.

Drew parked beside me in the front yard. The house was technically mine now, but I wasn't sure I'd ever think of it that way. When Gamma Rose was there, the place felt cozy. Now, it felt airless and lonesome. I also noticed how run-down the place looked. It needed painting, inside and out, and the carpet pattern was worn to extinction. Not that I'd thought about living here. I doubted anyone would without some major remodeling.

The front yard was sunny and cool, and the trees shone with color. Drew and I decided to eat our lunch outdoors. We sat on Gamma's wooden chairs, unwrapped our sandwiches, and set our drinks on an overturned five-gallon bucket. I heard a bluebird's soft warble and a squirrel scolding something below him on the ground—perhaps a snake or a stray cat. The gray pall I'd felt since Gamma's death began to lift from my shoulders.

Drew leaned back and crossed his feet in front of him. He had changed into sneakers but still wore his slacks and dress shirt from the funeral.

"So who is this guy you visited at the hospital?" he asked.

"He's a hospice worker who helped take care of Gamma Rose. He was great, actually, until he deserted us. Also tall and good looking." I gave him a cheesy smile.

"So you two have a thing going?" He wasn't smiling.

I rolled my eyes. "We do not have a thing going. I found him unconscious on Gamma's acreage when the sheriff came to recover the bones. He'd been shot in the leg. Most likely collateral damage from when somebody fired at me."

"What was he doing there?"

"Exactly what I'd like to know. But he was still sedated and couldn't talk." I chewed my veggie burger thoughtfully. "Also, I think he took Gamma's will from the house. Why would he do that?"

"Maybe an excuse to see you again."

I put down my sandwich and grinned at him. "You're jealous, aren't you?"

He nodded, self-deprecating. "Little bit, yeah."

Suddenly overcome with emotion, I got up and straddled his lap, nearly tipping over his chair, and planted a serious kiss on his mouth. He held his burger to one side, but it didn't take long for both arms to encircle my back. When I tried to pull away, he wasn't having it.

All the old feelings ignited. For a few lovely moments I forgot about the disturbing news about my health that I hadn't yet told him. When I remembered, my eyes filled.

He touched my temple. "What's this? Tears?"

"I am so glad you're here. There's something I need to tell you. And it isn't good."

I dismounted and moved back to my own chair.

While the sun plied its slow arc across the afternoon, I told him everything. We walked the winding driveway to the road, turned, and walked back again. I explained the doctor's prediction of my early death. I showed him the fence around Gamma Rose's acreage and told him about the bones on the mountain that did not belong to Pesha, who was my last hope of defying the mitochondrial curse. He listened, his eyes on the ground, frowning. Occasionally he asked for a clarification, but mostly he was silent.

We returned to our chairs in the front yard. We watched the woods darken and then the sky, while I told him about Zabella and the love affair between her son and my missing grandmother.

At last I ran out of words. Drew was quiet for a long time, his face tilted toward the emerging stars. Deep in the woods, an owl called to his mate. I propped my elbows on my knees and rubbed my eyes. When he finally spoke, it was his take-charge lawyer tone I remembered from the year we'd worked together back in Tetumka.

"The first thing we need to do is get a third opinion from a doctor who's a recognized authority on genetic defects. I'm sure we can find one in the City."

He meant New York City, not quite trusting medical expertise in small towns.

"Second, we find Pesha, or what happened to her, and how old she was if she died. I have a buddy who's an outstanding private investigator for our law firm. I know you can't afford him, but I can, and you have to let me do this. No arguments."

My nose was running. I dug a tissue from my pocket. "Drew—"

"No. My turn." He turned sideways in the wooden chair and took my shoulders in his hands. "I love you, Chantalene. I've tried to respect your need to establish your own identity after learning what happened to your parents. But I never intended to give up on us. In fact, I never intended to wait this long."

It was impossible not to meet his eyes. My lip trembled.

"Answer me this," he said. "If you'd never gone to that doctor, didn't know anything about this genetic defect, and I asked you to marry me right now, would you do it?"

I couldn't speak. I made a noise like a wounded goose.

"Would you?" he insisted.

My voice shook. "In one of your New York minutes."

He blew out a breath and smiled. "Okay then. That's all I need to know. I want to spend the rest of my life with you, no matter how long or how short. We'll take it one day at a time."

"But you want kids."

"Of course I do. At least one. Don't you? And we'll have that, God willing. If the worst happens and you don't get to see our children grown, do you trust me to raise them the way you'd want me to?"

I swallowed hard. "You'd be a wonderful dad. The best role model a child could have."

"Then stop denying happiness, for yourself and for me. We're wasting time that we should spend together."

I fell into his arms like a ninth-grade schoolgirl.

How could I be lucky enough to fall in love with a man like this? Or better yet, he with me? We spent the night on fresh sheets in Gamma Rose's bed making love. I was pretty sure she would approve.

WE WERE FEEDING the chickens the next morning when Drew heard the land line ring and jogged inside to answer. In a moment he stuck his head out the door.

"It's an attorney named Dell Sampson."

"Good!" I tossed the remaining feed and hurried to the phone.

"Sorry for the loss of your great-grandmother," he said. "She was quite a character, and I liked her."

"Thank you."

"My assistant has found a copy of Missus Tsura's will in our computer files. We'll print you a copy."

"Thank you. I'll stop by this afternoon, if that's okay."

"I'll be here."

Drew and I spent the morning cleaning out drawers, closets, and shelves. There's something vulture-like about going through a deceased person's things. The Romani, perhaps, were less sentimental. I thought of the woman at the funeral who'd advised me to burn Gamma's things or sell them to non-Romani. We piled old clothes, musty bedding, and see-through towels on a bare space in the front yard. Tonight we'd have a bonfire, Gypsy style.

Drew and I discussed whether I should sell the house or keep it as a getaway spot. I was concerned what might happen if it sat vacant most of the year. Either way, there was a lot of junk that needed to go.

I kept hoping to find something connected to Pesha, but even if I found such a thing, how would I know? I left basic dishes and pots and pans in the kitchen. The box of photos and a couple of her chicken tchotchkes went into my car, along with her walking stick.

For lunch we raided the refrigerator, then cleaned up and drove to town in Drew's car. He waited in the outer office while I stepped inside to see the attorney.

Dell Sampson was medium height with a dark complexion, perhaps some Middle-Eastern or Spanish heritage. He was not a smiler.

I extracted my photo ID and laid it on his desktop. He examined the name and picture and gave it back to me. "What happened to the original will?"

"I'm not sure." I shrugged. "Her mind was a bit hazy." Sorry, Gamma.

He handed me a manila envelope. "This copy, of course, doesn't have her signature. But should the need arise, I can attest that she did sign it here in my office, and my assistant was a witness."

"I appreciate that. I'm still hoping the original will turn up."

I glanced through the pages to make sure the will was the same one I had read. It appeared to be. I stuck it back inside the envelope.

"Mister Sampson, did you ever meet my grandmother, Pesha?"

He frowned. "No. There's no Pesha mentioned in the will."

"I know. She was Gamma Rose's daughter, and they were estranged. My mother was Pesha's daughter, and I need to know if Pesha's still living."

He seemed displeased by this. "Ms. Tsura didn't mention her daughter. I suppose the daughter could contest the will, if she knew about it."

"I'm not concerned about the will," I said. "It's for medical reasons."

"Ah, I see. Sorry I can't help."

I stood. "Thanks for your time. What do I owe you for this copy?"

He brushed away the idea. "Nothing at all. It's a few sheets of paper." Still no smile, even when he wasn't behaving like a lawyer.

"You're very kind." I turned to go.

"Have you asked the other person listed in the will about the daughter? This Zabella Mallosh. Is she some relation?"

So Gamma Rose hadn't explained the strange bequeath to her attorney either. "Not exactly," I said. "They were apparently..." co-conspirators "...good friends. Thank you, again."

Next we stopped by to see Sheriff Donovan, but he wasn't in.

"He's driving over to Mountain Home," Deputy Judy told us. "Do you have his mobile number?"

"I do. But I'm not sure I can get through on my cell if he's very far from town."

"Use the land line in his office," she said, pointing. "That'll work."

Small towns. Ya gotta love 'em.

I made myself comfortable behind the sheriff's desk, while Drew took a seat in the visitor's chair. I pushed the speakerphone button so he could listen.

On the second ring, a distinctive bass voice answered. "Donovan. What's up, Judy?"

"Actually, it's Chantalene Morrell. I stopped by your office to ask about the next step in identifying those bones."

"Miss Morrell. I've requested priority on the DNA, but the time frame depends on the backlog of other priority requests. I'll question that Jake fellow when he wakes up, but that's likely a separate issue."

I huffed out a breath. "Yeah, I guess so."

"By the way, we found his pickup pulled off the road in the brush about a quarter mile from your place. No apparent damage."

"Weird." Had he tried to hide it?

"I'll be working a case in Mountain Home for a day or two, but I'll let you know if I learn anything new," Donovan said.

"Okay. Thanks."

I hung up feeling discouraged. "Let's stop by the hospital," I said to Drew. "If the sheriff isn't going to be there when Jake is able to talk, I want to be there myself." I smiled sweetly. "This time you should come in and meet your competition."

FOURTEEN

I DIDN'T STOP at the nurses' station but went directly to Jake's room. Surely he was awake by now. The police guard's chair was empty, so I tapped on the partly open door. "Are you decent?"

A hoarse male voice answered. "Come in."

I stuck my head into the room and we made eye contact. He didn't seem surprised to see me.

"Hi, Chantalene."

He actually smiled. Pretty ballsy, considering he'd abandoned his duty to Gamma Rose.

Drew followed me inside. The room smelled of hospital food and adhesive bandages. Jake wore one of those charming, ventilated gowns and his face was the color of phlegm. His right leg lay on top of the sheet, immobilized in a sort of cage and elevated on several pillows. I almost felt sorry for him. But not quite.

Jake's eyes went immediately to the stranger in the room.

"This is Drew, my... fiancé." I stumbled over the word and Drew gave me a look. I still wasn't used to the idea that he'd proposed and I'd accepted.

"Pleased to meet you." Jake extended his hand, ever the gentleman.

Drew stepped closer and they shook. "You too, Jake. Looks like you're fairly well hobbled."

"Just another tricky day." Lines of stress, or pain, bracketed his smile. "I'm pretty good right now. They have me on pain killers."

That explained the slowness of his speech.

He turned to me. "I understand you rescued me. Thank you."

How could he be so cordial after what he'd done? Maybe that, too, was the painkillers. "Any idea who shot you?" I asked.

His head rolled from side to side on the pillow. "I was going to ask you the same thing. Your great-grandmother passed away right after you left. Very quick. I started up the mountain to find you, and the next thing I knew I heard a shot and my leg went out from under me."

The anguish on his face looked genuine. I frowned. "When I got back and you weren't there, I was really angry."

"I'm sorry. I guess I should have waited, but I thought you'd want to know as soon as possible."

My resentment ebbed. "Okay. But why did you take her will?"

His forehead creased. "What?"

I kept my voice firm. "Her will was gone. And you're the only one who'd been there."

"Her will to live? I don't understand."

"Her legal will, as in last will and testament. You were the only other person in the house. I want it back."

"I didn't even know she had a will. I didn't take anything." He was either truly confused or a Broadway-class actor.

"Then where did it go? Who else was there?"

"Nobody that I know of. Maybe someone came in after I went to find you."

This was something I had not considered. The window of time between the rifle shot and my skid down the mountain to the house was pretty slim. Maybe twenty minutes. Still, it could have been possible for somebody to slip into the house during that time. Unlikely, but possible.

I glanced at Drew. He was watching Jake closely, his face impassive.

"What about your truck?" I asked.

"I left the keys in it. Just move it, if it's in your way."

"Your truck wasn't there when I got back to the house."

This brought his head up from the pillow. "Somebody stole my truck?"

"A deputy found it pulled off the road in some brush about a quarter mile from Gamma Rose's house."

"Was it trashed?"

The pain on his face was more than physical. Never get between a man and his truck. Grudgingly, I believed his story. "No. And the keys were still in it."

His head flopped back on the pillow. "This is nuts. I need to get out of this place."

"I don't think they'll release you for a while."

"Not the hospital. I need to get out of Arkansas." He closed his eyes, his breath heavy. "I moved down here from Missouri because my dad once told me he had family around here. I thought maybe I could find them."

At the mention of Missouri, my attention perked up. "No luck?"

"Nobody I've talked to recognized his name. I checked Google and the county courthouse. Even the phonebook doesn't list anybody with the last name of Wayne."

"What was your father's first name?"

"Ian," he said.

Chill bumps raced up my arms. That wasn't a common name in these hills. It would make sense if Zabella's son changed his last name to avoid detection when he and my grandmother ran north.

"Were his people Romani?"

"No idea. He never mentioned that."

I paused a moment, remembering my visit to Zabella's living room. "Was your dad a fan of Western movies?"

Jake's eyes widened. "How in the world did you know that? Do you have a mole on your tongue, too?"

"No. But maybe the gift runs in the family."

He sighed and pushed the call button for his nurse. "I need another pain pill."

I took the hint. "I'll check on you tomorrow. And don't worry about your truck being vandalized. The sheriff impounded it."

This did not seem to cheer him up. He grimaced and closed his eyes.

Drew and I passed the nurse in the hallway. We retraced our path to the hospital entrance without talking, but it was hard to contain myself. Outside the glass doors, I grabbed his shirt.

"Ian was Zabella's son's name! I'll bet he changed his last name so nobody could find them. He loved Westerns and named himself after John Wayne!"

"Whoa," he said, laughing. "That's quite a stretch, pardner."

"I know. But that doesn't mean it's wrong."

MY SPIDEY-SENSE was vibrating. I felt I was close to learning Pesha's fate, and I couldn't wait to talk to Jake again. Maybe next time he would be clear-headed.

Drew wanted to call his office while we still had cell reception. We walked to a grassy area on the hospital grounds and sat on a stone bench beside a fountain. A marble St. Francis offered seeds to the birds. Chrysanthemums nodded their yellow heads in the sunshine.

He also phoned a friend and got the name of a hotshot doctor in New York. He scheduled the first available appointment for me, which was a month out. Then he booked my flight from Oklahoma City to LaGuardia. He would pick me up and go with me to see the doctor.

I acquiesced, though the whole plan made me uncomfortable. Not just because of the flying, but also because lately I didn't have a high opinion of doctors. They tended to tell me things I didn't want to hear. But Drew was a fixer. It was a trait I'd have to get used to. He did agree to hold off contacting his PI friend until I could ask Jake his mother's name and the town where they lived. Pesha might have changed her name, but I would bring a picture for him to identify.

Drew read my anxiety and grabbed my hand. "Let's take a walk."

We strolled around the building a few times, which didn't take long. He suggested I retain Dell Sampson to handle legal details of Gamma Rose's estate, including the transfer of her twenty acres to Zabella and the house to me. Drew was a corporate attorney specializing in tax law, and he assured me that since her holdings were small, no estate tax or inheritance tax would be required. I appreciated his guidance.

We put off making wedding plans until I came to New York. I was definitely not a big-wedding gal, nor did I have family to invite. I didn't know what Drew might prefer, but I pictured a destination wedding for just the two of us. Somewhere with palm trees and turquoise water. But right now, we had an estate to settle and a mystery to solve. I was exceedingly glad to have an accomplice.

With those boxes checked, we stopped by the funeral parlor to settle up with Mr. Matthews. Gamma Rose's savings account held just enough money to pay for the service. "No charge for the parade," he said through his voice amplifier and smiled.

I wanted to go back to the hospital from there and question Jake again, but Drew talked me down.

"Let's give him time to rest," he said. "It's not as if he's going anywhere. Besides, we have to drive back to the house and get the photo you want to show him." He draped his arm across my shoulders. "Then let's have dinner someplace nice to celebrate our de facto engagement."

"I get hot when you talk like a lawyer," I said. He pinched my ribs. "Dinner sounds great. Your treat. And afterward, we can stop by the hospital."

"I promise."

DREW RESERVED A table at a restaurant that was five miles out of Madison. The building nestled in an elbow of mountain scenery that was truly spectacular. We were seated in an outdoor courtyard, sheltered from the wind and warmed by standing heaters that looked like tall mushrooms. The courtyard overlooked a small lake.

I was still hopped up to show Jake the photo of Pesha. At first I was too nervous to enjoy my pasta primavera smothered in grated parmesan, even though it tasted fabulous. After a glass of wine, though, my shoulders relaxed and my appetite returned. I don't drink often, so when I do, I get the full effect. And right now, that was fine with me.

I ordered a second glass.

Drew looked even sexier than usual in a cashmere sweater the color of aged whiskey, his hair rumpled just enough to make me think of beds with cool sheets. Heat migrated up my neck, not from the wine alone. A feeling of well-being spread through my limbs, and my head felt giddy. It was the first time I'd felt happy since that grim doctor's visit back in Oklahoma.

"How did you manage to find this place?" I asked. "It's perfect."

"Trip Advisor and Google Earth," he said and winked.

He was handsome and smart! I was so lucky and out of my league! Then he cut into a rare steak that bled under his knife. I looked away quickly and focused on the inside of my wine glass, close-up. When we were married, we'd have to work out some compromises in the kitchen.

The waiter appeared with an ice bucket and champagne, on the house. His hair was oiled back like an Italian mobster and his flourish said angling-for-a-big-tip.

"Rumor has it that you are celebrating your engagement," he said in an accent I couldn't place. Southern Kentucky? Eastern Walmart?

I beamed. "We are!"

He placed two slender glasses on the table and poured. Then he replaced the white napkin over his arm and bowed. "Congratulations on your special occasion."

When the waiter had gone, Drew's expression sobered. "I'll buy you an engagement ring when you come to New York. With a diamond as big as you want."

"You will not," I said. "Think of all the travel and fun we could have with that amount of money. I want memories, not crushed carbon."

He smiled. "Maybe you can have both."

I raised my eyebrows. "You're doing that well in New York?"

"Pretty darned well, yeah. That's the only reason I took the job. That, and the woman I loved rejected me."

"You should have told me about the money," I said, smirking. "You buried the lede."

His laugh sounded like riches to me. The other two couples in the courtyard glanced at us and smiled. I leaned dangerously over the table and he met my lips without hesitation.

We drank the champagne. Then had coffee and shared a crème brûlée. By the time we left the restaurant, I was ready for bed but not sleep.

Instead, Drew drove me to the hospital as he'd promised. More character in his little finger than most men had in their entire souls.

At the prospect that Jake might identify Pesha as his mother, I sobered up fast.

FIFTEEN

JAKE HELD THE photo I handed him and looked into the eyes of a defiant, dark-haired teenager. The girl stared back at him.

"My mother's name wasn't Pesha, and her hair was red." He glanced up at me. "But she dyed her hair, maybe she changed her name, too. I'm ninety percent sure this is her."

My heart nearly stopped. "Is she still alive?"

He shrugged. "I don't know. She was never quite right after my father's death. When I'd try to talk to her, she looked at me like I was a stranger. One day she just got in the car and left. Didn't even take her clothes."

I saw pain in his eyes when he gave the photo back to me.

"I assume she's dead," he said. "If she was alive, surely she would have contacted me at some point, even if she didn't want to come home."

Maybe not, I thought. Apparently Pesha loved Ian more than her children. She abandoned a baby daughter to be with him, then her son after Ian died. I was caught between awe for that kind of love and outrage about those desertions. If indeed Jake's mother was Pesha. I wished he was one hundred percent sure instead of ninety.

His gaze shifted out the hospital window. "When I was a kid, she used to sing while she worked in the kitchen. Her voice was beautiful. After dad died she never sang again."

Gamma Rose had told me Pesha's voice was magic. This had to be the same woman. "How old were you when she left?"

"Sixteen. I thought she'd just gone to the store or to run errands. When she didn't come back that first night, I was really scared. But my dad had hammered into my head to never go to the police, for any reason. So I didn't."

I shook my head, speechless.

"I didn't have any money, but at least the house was paid for. I got a job stocking groceries on nights and weekends so I could finish school," he said. "A neighbor lady used to check on me and bring meals sometimes. If it hadn't been for her kindness, I'd probably have come to a bad end. She pressured the school counselor to find me a scholarship for college. When she passed away, that's when I started thinking about the relatives Dad mentioned in Arkansas." He looked away, his eyes shiny.

I gave him a few seconds. "Any idea where your mother went?"

"Not a clue. I was so angry and hurt that I never tried to find her. I figured if she didn't care what happened to me, I didn't care what happened to her."

"I'm sorry, Jake."

He nodded, his jaw tightening. "Why are you looking for her?"

He didn't need to know about my health issue, but he had a right to know about the family he had come here to find. "The photo is Gamma Rose's daughter who disappeared. My grandmother."

"Wait. My mother was your grandmother?"

His whole face opened. Whether it was shock or pleasure, I couldn't tell. Maybe both.

"What does that make us—some kind of cousins?" he asked.

This hadn't occurred to me yet. Wow.

If Pesha was his mother, he was a half-brother to my mom. I smiled. "I think you're my uncle. Or half uncle, if there's such a thing. My mom was your sister, by a different father."

Jake smiled back. In the space of a few minutes, we both had found family we never knew we had. I got a little misty and started laughing.

During this sappy scene, Drew sat quietly in a corner of the room. I turned to him. "I have an uncle!"

He smiled, but as always, he kept his eye on the ball. "So Jake, how old was your mother when she left?"

"She never would tell anybody her age, or even her birthday," he said. "But I do know she was really young when I was born. I'd guess that when I was sixteen, she was early to mid-thirties."

That was about the life span the doctor projected. Perhaps Pesha's depression wasn't caused by grief alone. She might have been ill.

"I didn't know she had another child," Jake said. "Was she unmarried?"

"No. She had an arranged marriage that didn't end well," I said.

Actually, I didn't know if it did end. Unless those bones on Gamma's land belonged to her first husband. A shiver flickered between my shoulder blades.

The DNA tests might show if the bones and I were related. I wondered if there was evidence of a gunshot wound. If the dead man was Tobar Kaldera, I'd rather think he was shot and fell into the crevasse instead of falling and perhaps not dying for days. He might have been a son-of-a-bitch, but he was also my grandfather.

The death could have been an accident. But if it wasn't, that would explain the collusion between Gamma Rose and Zabella to keep everyone off that property. They might have been covering up a murder.

A nurse came in to change the dressing on Jake's leg, so Drew and I said goodbye and made a quick escape.

I settled into the bucket seat of Drew's rental car, my head buzzing from the near miss of learning what happened to my grandmother. By the time we pulled up to Gamma's house, it was 10:30 p.m. The bonfire would have to wait. We were tired and ready for bed.

I lay next to him with my eyes open, watching leaf shadows toss on the ceiling. "I'm ready to hire your investigator to find Pesha. Now that we have a time frame and location, he'll have someplace to start. I can ask Jake for his old address and what kind of car Pesha was driving."

"I'll call Chad tomorrow," Drew said. "And let's get Dell Sampson started on the legal work. The sooner you execute the deeds for her land and house, the sooner you can go home."

I turned over so we lay face to face, looking into each other's eyes. "I can't go home until I find out who died on Gamma's land. How he got there, and why she was hiding his death."

"I get that. But I'm not sure there's anyone left who can tell you."

Not unless Jake and I teamed up on Zabella. I kept that idea to myself. I was certain she knew more than she'd told me. Did she know she had a grandson? If not, the chance to meet Jake might pry the truth out of her.

Drew's voice was soft in the darkness. "My flight out of Little Rock is the day after tomorrow. I'll have to leave here early to catch it."

"Oh, no." I had conveniently ignored the fact that at some point he would have to go back. "Can you put it off?"

"I wish. The partners are already pissed because I postponed a deposition."

The thought of his leaving made my breath heavy. I relived the memory of the last time he'd left for New York. I didn't see him again for many months and spent most of that time wishing he would come back.

To avoid whining, I changed the subject. "If we get married, where will we live?"

"When we get married," he said. "We'll live someplace that suits us both. Maybe more than one place. You should definitely keep your farm."

Farm was a euphemism for the sixty acres where I'd grown up. It was originally eighty acres, but I'd had to sell part of it a long time ago when I was broke. The farm was all I had left of my parents. Still, my perspective had changed in the past few weeks.

"I like the sound of home being more than one place," I said. "But I can live anywhere as long as we're together. Even New York."

He put his arms around me and pulled me close.

IN THE SMALL hours of the night, I awoke to the sound of a car engine. We were too far from the main road to hear traffic from there. This vehicle was coming up the driveway.

Drew was sleeping soundly and I didn't want to wake him. Made brave by his presence, I slipped out of bed, found my flip-flops, and sneaked to the front window. Headlights flashed through the trees and then went out.

Beneath the canopy of branches that hung over the driveway, I could barely see the car but I could hear it. I grabbed Gamma Rose's shotgun and flashlight. The shotgun wasn't loaded and probably wouldn't fire if it was. But my nocturnal visitor wouldn't know that. This time I was determined to find out who it was.

I opened the front door slowly and counted on the darkness inside to make me invisible. With the butt of the shotgun propped against my right shoulder, I held the barrel and the flashlight with my left hand, waiting for the car to appear in the open dooryard. The night was clear with a three-quarter moon. Enough light that I should be able to tell if it was the same vehicle as before.

It was. A dark SUV rolled very slowly into the yard, the engine idling. When it was close enough for the driver to see our cars parked to one side, the vehicle stopped and began to back up.

I yelled for Drew, and at the same time switched on the flashlight and burst out the door.

Shotgun raised, I jogged toward the car. "Stay where you are or I'll shoot!"

The flashlight beam was scarcely better than a candle in the shadow of the trees. I'd forgotten to put in new batteries after my last outing. The filmy light reflected from the vehicle's dented hood but did nothing to illuminate the interior.

The driver called my bluff and curved into a three-point turn. I stalked closer. "Stop! Who are you?"

I glimpsed the profile of a hooded sweatshirt. The tires spun dirt and the car lurched down the driveway, bucking over the ruts.

I dropped the weenie flashlight and gave chase. When it was obvious I couldn't catch up, I grasped the shotgun by the barrel, drew back my arm, and hurled it end over end at the taillights, screaming.

The car was already in the shadows, but I heard the shotgun hit the back window and career off the bumper into the trees. The driver gunned it and disappeared around the curve.

"Damn it, damn it, damn it!"

Drew appeared beside me in pajama bottoms. "What the hell?"

I was panting and sputtering like a madwoman. "I couldn't see the driver! But it was the same SUV as last time!"

"Last time? It's been here before?"

"Yeah. The second night I was here. It's like they don't expect anyone to be home. When they see a car, they take off." I puffed, trying to catch my breath.

"Burglars, maybe," he said.

"Maybe." But why would burglars target a house that so obviously didn't contain anything valuable?

He put his arm around my shoulders. "Come inside before we freeze."

I was wearing only the tee-shirt top of his pajamas and beginning to shiver. I retrieved the shotgun from the brush. It had a few new scars but nothing fatal. "I should load this thing and see if it actually fires."

"Tomorrow, Annie Oakley," he said. "Right now let's go back to bed."

There was no sleep for me. My mind pulled up random facts that I couldn't explain. Nighttime visits from a dark vehicle. A man's bones on the mountain. Red roses from an unknown sender. Gamma's missing will. An uncle I'd never known about, shot in the leg. My heartbeat battered against my ears.

WHEN I AWOKE it was full daylight and the room smelled like smoke. I sat straight up in the bed. Drew wasn't there.

I pulled on sweat pants and trotted to the living room window. He was overseeing the pile of burning debris we'd collected from the house. A garden hose snaked along the ground beside him, in case the fire overstepped its prescribed boundaries. I didn't even know we had a hose.

Drew had also made coffee. Mug in hand, I walked out to the front yard. Fingers of flame curled from the edges of threadbare quilts and yellowed pillows. Smoke spiraled upward and dissolved into blue sky. It smelled awful.

He looked up and smiled. "Good morning. Perfect day for burning."

It was in fact a stunning day. Bright sunshine, cool air, scarcely a breeze. Birds and squirrels gossiping in the trees. And a sexy man in jeans and sleeveless tee, looking good enough to ravish.

With gallant restraint, I settled for a hug. "I could get used to somebody getting up early and making me coffee," I said. "I think I'll keep you."

"I'll hang around on the condition you fix breakfast."

"Fair enough. I'll feed the girls and check for eggs."

I moseyed over to the chicken yard and let Penny and Midnight out of their pen. In exchange for food and fresh water, they provided two brown eggs. I decided to make pancakes for Drew. The idea made me happy.

The morning was so innocently bucolic that the strange car in the night now felt unreal. For a moment I wondered if I had dreamed the whole incident. But as I walked toward the house, there was a reminder—on the packed ground lay the flashlight where I'd dropped it during the chase. I replayed the episode in detail. It was like being stalked, both frightening and infuriating. I would report it to Sheriff Donovan, but what could he do? It wasn't against the law to troll through someone's driveway in the middle of the night.

After breakfast, we finished our burning project and hosed down the ashes. Drew texted his investigator friend and asked him to call our land line. How his texts could get through when phone calls couldn't was a technological mystery.

While he waited for an answer, I made appointments to see the sheriff and Dell Sampson in Madison. We reserved the evening hours to spend privately on what would be our last night together for quite a while.

When the PI called back, Drew talked to him for a few minutes and then handed me the phone. The investigator had questions about my family that Drew couldn't answer. Mostly, I couldn't either, but I did my best. Chad Epperson sounded fiftyish, whip-smart and hard-nosed, but polite. Good qualities for a PI, I thought. Drew would probably pay an outlandish sum for his services, but he wouldn't discuss that. I decided to give up feeling guilty.

That afternoon we drove to town. I signed papers and asked questions of Dell Sampson.

"We should be able to settle things quickly," he said. "I'll prepare a warranty deed for the twenty acres. You and Ms. Mallosh will both need to sign."

I wondered how that would go. But since it benefitted Zabella, I had a hunch she would cooperate.

We discussed the possibility of renting Gamma's house versus letting it sit vacant if I didn't want to sell it right away. "I'm concerned because twice somebody has driven out there in the middle of the night, but they left when they saw the house was occupied," I said.

"It is quite isolated. I'd worry too," he agreed. "Plus, a house deteriorates fast when it sits vacant. I can recommend a real estate agent who could manage the property and find a dependable renter, if you want."

"I'd appreciate that."

He scratched the agency name and phone number on a piece of paper and handed it to me. "Ask for Sheryl."

I smiled. "A member of the family, I presume?"

"Sister-in-law," he said, straight-faced. Humor was lost on Dell Sampson.

From the attorney's office we drove to see Sheriff Donovan. In his crowded office, the sheriff leaned back dangerously in his spring-loaded desk chair.

"I checked with the lab this morning," he said. "They actually took to heart my request for priority on the DNA. Said they'd fax the results by five this afternoon."

All three of us glanced at the clock. Three p.m.

We couldn't sit in his office for two more hours. Presumably he had other work to do. But I wasn't going back home until that report came in.

"Do you know if the pathologist suggested a cause of death? Like a gunshot wound?"

"Not that was visible. I asked that specifically. Possibly a broken neck. The head was separated, but that could have happened a number of ways over the years."

I tried not to picture what those ways were, but my mind flashed an image of slavering coyotes. I told the sheriff about the dark gray SUV.

"Did you get the tag number?"

I shook my head. "It was too dark. But I could tell it was a Ford, and really old."

"That's pretty general. If we searched for old Ford SUVs in the county license tag records, there'd be hundreds. Wouldn't narrow it down much."

"What about the person who shot Jake? Any clues?"

"Doc found the bullet in his leg. Trouble is, everybody and his pet monkey has a rifle around here. Still, it's a lead."

It was a pro forma question anyway. I knew good and well who fired that shot, but with no proof except a vague confession she'd probably deny, I stopped short of accusing her.

Reluctantly, I stood and glanced at Drew. "Let's go kill some time and check back with the sheriff at five."

"I have your cell number," Sheriff Donovan said. "I'll give you a buzz when the fax comes in."

We walked through the reception office and Drew had his hand on the door when a warbling ringtone sounded from a machine in the corner.

"Hang on a minute," the sheriff said. "That's the fax machine."

The machine shifted gears and began to groan. Not exactly state of the art, but then most fax machines were obsolete these days.

The lady deputy stood over the machine while it produced a series of pages. When it stopped grinding, she handed the pages to the sheriff. He took so long reading them that I began to squirm.

"Well? What's it say?"

Sheriff Donovan sucked his teeth. "Inconclusive. If the bones were from a female, they could check for a match with mitochondrial DNA. But since they're from a male, the common genetic test can't effectively identify a relationship with your DNA."

"They couldn't even tell if we're related?"

"Apparently not. And the bones are too old for the DNA to show up in a national database."

"What about using dental records to identify him?"

"Whoever this guy was, he had perfect teeth. Not one filling." He rolled the papers and slapped them against his leg. "In other words, we've got bupkis. Unless a witness comes forward—if there is one that's still alive—we may never know who that fella was."

I had my suspicions, but again, no proof.

SIXTEEN

ON OUR LAST night together, texts pinged repeatedly on Drew's phone, drawing his attention to the pending litigation that awaited him in New York.

My mind, too, was scattered. It turned out that a mitochondrial defect wasn't the only flaw in my genetic makeup. My maternal grandparents were both scoundrels, to put it kindly. My mother was lucky to be raised by Gamma Rose instead of her parents.

I agreed with Jake that Pesha was most likely dead. But at what age, and what was the cause? The answers were vitally important to my future with Drew. I didn't want to spend the rest of my life, however long or short it might be, waiting to be ambushed. Living one day at a time was a lofty philosophy that I'd never been able to embrace. For good or ill, I was a planner.

Drew would have to leave by three a.m. to make his mid-day flight out of Little Rock. The airport was a three-hour drive, and that didn't allow for traffic or road construction. I was extremely grateful that he had come. It spoke to his seriousness about being my partner for life. I just wished I had more certainty about how long that might be.

But as Thelma had pointed out, no one had that certainty.

We retired early and made love, slow and easy to make it last. Afterward, we both pretended to sleep, hoping not to disturb the other. The woods were quiet, no owl calls, no wind to rattle the fallen leaves. I listened to the minutes tick by in silence.

At 2:45 a.m. the sky was ink black and peppered with stars as we stood in the yard beside his rental car and hugged fiercely. Condensation trickled down the car's windows and a cosmic emptiness yawned in my chest. For months I'd been learning how to live without him, but that skill vanished the moment he appeared in the chapel. I harbored a secret terror that these few idyllic days were too good to be true.

He held me by the shoulders and looked into my eyes. "I'll see you in New York one month from today." Tiny moons floated in his dilated pupils. "Let's drive up the coast for a pre-honeymoon somewhere out of the city, make our plans from there."

I did my best to smile. "It's a date."

He gave me a kiss and slid into the driver's seat. The engine sounded loud in the night. He waved one last time as he drove away.

Alone in the dark, I watched his taillights disappear, listening until the sound of his leaving was only a whisper in the night. Then I went inside, crawled back under the covers, and settled into the curve that was still warm from Drew's body.

MY SLUMBER WAS peculiar and shallow. Just before dawn, I roused to that stupefied state between awake and asleep and sensed someone was in the room. But I couldn't open my eyes and my limbs felt weighted.

"Who's there?"

I thought I'd spoken aloud but wasn't sure. The words were thick on my tongue. I heard no response but somehow became aware that the presence was familiar.

"Gamma Rose?"

Her spirit bloomed like a cloud, though I couldn't see her.

Stay off the mountain. It is cursed. Bolime! Bad luck.

"Did someone kill Tobar?" I asked. "The bones are his, aren't they?"

Go back to Oklahoma where you are safe.

I frowned, clenching my fists. "Why is the mountain cursed? Why won't you tell me what happened?"

A powerful current swept through the room then, sucking the oxygen from my lungs. I gasped and my eyes flashed opened. I lay there panting, my pulse like hoof beats in my ears.

Predawn light seeped through the curtains. No one else was there. I didn't know whether I had been awake or dreaming, or if Gamma Rose's powers extended beyond the grave.

I sat up and took deep breaths to clear my head. A cold irony coated my skin. Like my great-grandmother, I was speaking to the unseen.

THOROUGHLY UNNERVED, I arose and made coffee. I dressed in jeans and a flannel shirt, fed the chickens, and wasted no time leaving the house.

An orange sun hovered on the horizon when I reached the hospital on the near edge of Madison. I stepped off the elevator at Jake's floor and was surprised to see him coming down the hall on crutches. At his side was a pretty nurse I hadn't seen before. She was holding onto a wide belt fastened around his middle to steady him.

He saw me and smiled, despite the pain lines creasing his forehead. "If it isn't my long-lost niece. Good morning."

"Look at you. You're vertical again."

"Thank goodness. I'm wobbly and can't put any weight on the leg. Otherwise, I'm ready to go hiking."

His nurse giggled. No surprise if she was smitten with her lanky, well-built patient in his skimpy flowered gown. Hard to put on pants over that hip cast. When I'd broken my leg, I spent eight weeks in skirts, but I doubted Jake would go for that.

I stepped to one side while Jake and his sidekick continued to the end of the hall and turned around. He maneuvered the crutches with an athletic confidence I had never achieved. Go Jake. I wondered how he would manage when he went home and his large dog leapt for joy.

Back in his room, the nurse settled him in the blanket-lined recliner and spread another blanket over his bare leg. Then she left to make her rounds. Jake's hair was rumpled and his face showed his true age for the first time since I'd met him. Being physically fit didn't spare him from pain. Swinging that damaged leg in a bulky cast had to hurt like the dickens.

Still, he was in good spirits. "The doc says I might get to go home tomorrow," he said.

"Really! That's great news. Do you have someone to help out, bring in food and stuff? You won't be able to drive for quite a while." I nearly bit my tongue when I realized that, as a relative, he might expect me to step up. If I declined, I'd be riddled with guilt. "I guess I could do that...."

"That's good of you. But my insurance will pay for home health. Since there's no rehab center in town, I'll have a visiting nurse and a physical therapist." His smile skewed. "Kind of like being on hospice."

"What goes around does come around." I took a seat on the foot of the bed. "I'll be going back to Oklahoma soon, but until then I can stop by once in a while, unless you'd rather I didn't."

"I'd rather you did. I'll be stuck in the house and bored to a crisp." He hesitated. "There is a favor I need, if you would."

"What's that?"

"I need some workout clothes from my house. A pair of sweat pants and a tee shirt to wear home. I can't leave here in this ridiculous gown."

I smiled. "Sure. Where's your house?"

He named a street unfamiliar to me and I put the address in my phone.

"It's here in town. Your GPS should find it," he said. "There's a key above the doorjamb."

"Do you need a ride home from the hospital?"

"I might, if home health doesn't cover that. Thanks." He tugged the blanket back over his leg. "The sheriff stopped by. He says there's not much chance of figuring out who shot me. It was probably accidental."

I nodded. "Most likely." Because she was aiming at me.

I fiddled with my purse strap. "Jake, you met one of your grandmothers, even though you didn't know it when you were helping with Gamma Rose. Would you like to meet your other one? Ian's mother."

His eyes widened. "You know her? She lives around here?"

"Yes. Her name is Zabella Mallosh. Zabella told me she had a son named Ian who ran away with my grandmother Pesha—while she was still married to a man she hated."

He shook his head. "Wow. I always thought I had such normal parents. Turns out I didn't even know who they were. I sure didn't know about her first husband."

"Pesha never wanted to marry him, and I'm told he abused her. In that time and culture, I guess there was no penalty for spousal abuse."

"Then I can't blame her for running away."

"I agree. But she left behind a baby girl who was my mother."

He just shook his head.

"The day you went to find me on the mountain, I found human bones that had been there many years. I suspect they might be her first husband."

He grimaced. "Good grief, this just gets better and better. You don't think he was murdered, do you?"

"I don't know. But it's hard to see why else he'd end up in a chasm in the rocks. And why Gamma Rose and Zabella worked in concert to keep those bones hidden." I paused. "I'm sorry, Jake. I know this is a lot."

"You don't think my dad…? He was such a gentle soul. I can't believe he would have done such a thing."

"People do surprising things for love. Both wonderful and terrible."

He was quiet a minute or two and I didn't interrupt his thoughts. I'd had time to adjust to my outré family history, but it was all new to Jake.

"Does my grandmother know I exist?" he asked.

I shrugged. "She claimed she didn't hear from your father after they ran away, but she wasn't telling me the whole story. I think she's the only one left who actually knows the truth. When you're up to it, I can take you to meet her if you want."

"I do." He nodded. "I came here to learn about my family. The good, the bad, and the ugly."

FROM THE HOSPITAL I drove downtown, if you could called it that, to Dell Sampson's storefront office. I parked in a slanted spot by the street and went inside.

Business must have been slow because he'd already examined Gamma's abstract and certified the title to the twenty acres, which was separate from the house. His assistant, Janelle, had prepared a warranty deed transferring the title to Zabella. As executor of her estate, I would sign for Gamma Rose.

"We've made three copies. For you, Missus Mallosh, and for recording at the county courthouse. The signatures must be notarized. Let's make an appointment for the two of you to come in. Janelle is a notary."

I thanked him for the swift work. "I don't have a phone number for Zabella, but I'm going to visit her soon. I'll phone you to set a time."

"Excellent."

I stood, shook the hand he offered, and left his office.

Late that afternoon Drew texted that he'd arrived on time in NYC. Since it was before five p.m., he had gone straight to his office from the airport. Sometimes his work ethic exasperated me.

On Gamma Rose's kitchen calendar I started crossing off the days until I'd see him again.

SEVENTEEN

THE NEXT MORNING I drove to Jake's house. It was a small white clapboard with neatly clipped shrubs across the front, but no flowers in the front bed. When I shut the car door, baritone barking erupted from the fenced backyard. That must be T-Bone.

I found the key and let myself in. The interior looked like a bachelor's place, but a neat bachelor. No beer cans on the coffee table nor laundry on the floor. A super-sized TV took up one wall of the living room, and one of the two bedrooms was full of exercise equipment. His flowered bedspread was a shock, but he redeemed his masculinity by leaving the bed unmade.

In a bureau drawer I found a pair of gray sweats and a Nature Conservancy tee shirt. They were actually folded. He hadn't asked for underwear or socks, but I added those to the pile. This wasn't weird, right, because he was family.

Suddenly, I heard toenails on a hard floor. Before I could move, I received a vigorous nudge in the derriere. I shrieked. T-Bone apparently thought that was funny because when I whirled around, he gave me a sloppy grin and barked. His tongue lolled half a foot out of his mouth.

Obviously, there was a doggie door somewhere in the house. The mutt was huge but harmless. He burrowed his forehead into my stomach, his tail a furry metronome. Poor guy was obviously lonely. I scratched behind his ears and talked to him in a low voice. He gave tiny whines of delight that made me laugh. No wonder Jake was so crazy about him.

"Want to go home with me, boy? You could have fun chasing the chickens around the yard." For a few minutes I actually thought about taking him, but Jake said he might come home tomorrow.

It was a struggle to get out the front door with Jake's clothes but without the dog. With the door closed, I heard him whining on the other side and felt bad about leaving him. I checked the backyard to make sure he had food and water. He did, along with a variety of chew toys and old tennis balls. T-Bone might be lonesome but he wasn't deprived.

It was almost ten o'clock when I arrived at the hospital. The doctor was just leaving Jake's room.

"They're discharging me this morning," he announced.

"Congratulations. Your dog will be deliriously happy."

He grinned. "You met T-Bone, did you?"

"He's hard to miss."

A nurse came in with his paperwork. "Let's go over your instructions and get you dressed," she said.

"Here are his clothes." I laid my bundle on the bed and turned on my heel. Helping Jake put his pants on was a bridge too far.

I followed the smell of coffee down the hall while picturing the contortions required to pull sweatpants over his cast. I'd nearly finished a cup when the nurse finally emerged from his room, looking undaunted and holstering a pair of scissors.

"You can move your car to the breezeway in front," she said. "I'll bring him down in a wheelchair."

Apparently I was driving him home.

I retrieved my CRV from the parking lot and pulled under the overhang by the front doors. On the passenger-side, I pushed the seat back as far as it would go and left the door open. When Jake and the nurse came out, he didn't look happy about riding in a wheelchair or having one leg of his sweatpants chopped off at mid-thigh.

"Ah. A wardrobe adjustment," I said. He grunted.

He transferred himself onto the car seat with the nurse's help, and they angled his cast into the floorboard. It was no easy task. She set his crutches and bag of hospital supplies in the back and wished him well. I pulled out of the driveway and onto the main road.

"Don't pay the ransom. I've escaped!" he said and huffed out a sigh. "Can't wait to sleep in my own bed."

"I'll bet. Once you're settled, I can pick up some groceries, if you like."

"That'd be great. Mainly stuff I can microwave." He glanced over at me. "I really appreciate your help. But don't feel obligated just because we turned out to be related."

"I don't. You were kind to Gamma Rose, and she liked you."

He nodded, accepting this quid pro quo. "So when are we going to meet this woman who's allegedly my other grandmother?"

He probably wondered why this made me laugh. I couldn't wait to tell Zabella that she'd shot her own grandson. "How about after lunch?"

JAKE'S REUNION WITH T-Bone was touching and dangerous. The dog waited just inside the front door, hopping and yipping and slobbering. I thought sure he would knock the crutches out from under Jake. But he managed to keep his balance, leaning forward to massage the dog's head. T-Bone's tail wagged violently.

I ran interference while Jake made his way to a recliner in the living room. T-Bone wanted to jump in his lap but settled for sniffing every inch of the leg cast. Jake gave me cash and directions to a food market. The two of them were snuggling as I headed to the store.

I sacked up fruits and vegetables that wouldn't require cooking and selected he-man-sized frozen dinners that purported to be healthy. Bread, milk, peanut butter, and a six-pack of beer. Everything the sophisticated bachelor could need.

He was born after my mother, which would put him in his late forties. To me he felt more like a cousin than an uncle. But what did I know about it? I'd never had either of those. I was still searching for a comfort zone with our kinship. The fact that we were blood relation connected me to the world in a way I thought I'd lost when Gamma Rose died. Luckily, I liked him.

A block down from the grocery store, a sign outside the Good Eats Café advertised homemade chili. A perfect lunch for a nippy October day. There was only one parking space left, which spoke well for the food. I bought two bowls of chili to go, beef for Jake and veggie for me.

We ate at the dinette table in his kitchen. He spooned up his chili like a man who'd been subsisting on bland hospital food for a week.

"This is really good," he said.

To my surprise, T-Bone sat like a good boy and watched us eat without begging. But his head tracked back and forth with every bite Jake took. When we'd finished, I threw away the Styrofoam bowls, rinsed our spoons and glasses, and loaded them in the dishwasher.

"Don't get used to this kind of service," I told him.

"Well shoot. Can't get good help anymore." He stretched out his uninjured leg and tried to straighten his back.

"You need a pain pill?"

"No, I'm okay."

"You sure you're ready to go meet your grandmother? The roads out that way are pretty bumpy."

He gathered his crutches. "Ready as I'll ever be."

The sheriff had arranged for Jake's truck to be delivered to his house, but he wasn't cleared to drive. I declined to shepherd that behemoth over windy narrow roads. So we crammed him back into my car and took off.

After a while he began to recognize landmarks. "This is the same way I came to your great-grandmother's house," he said.

"Yep. Turns out Zabella lives next door. If you can count a half mile as next door."

I found her tree-shrouded driveway, and we jounced along the two-track lane toward her patch-quilt house. The rough ride must have hurt Jake's leg, but he suffered in silence.

I parked in the dooryard. Jake didn't react to her strange-looking residence. I supposed he'd made enough home visits as a hospice worker that not much surprised him. The old Cadillac still sat in the parking area, decomposing under a layer of dust. Zabella's thread-bare mutts barked without rising from their dusty depressions behind the Caddie's flat tires.

"What's her name again?" he asked.

"Zabella Mallosh. She lives alone as far as I can tell. She told me she had two daughters, but Ian was the only son and apparently her favorite. She's a canny old girl and very blunt."

He nodded and opened his door. "Here goes nothing."

I rapped on Zabella's front door while Jake stood back, shoulders rounded over his crutches. "The nurse should have adjusted those things for you," I said. "I'll fix them when we get back to your place."

No one answered. I knocked again.

Finally Zabella appeared in the doorway. "You again," she said, ignoring Jake. "What do you want?"

"Nice to see you, too. My friend wants to meet you." I gave her a sunny smile. "He's Ian and Pesha's son."

She scowled as if this was a crude joke, but then her gaze traveled to Jake. She examined him from cast to crutches to the handsome face, and there her eyes stopped. I saw the moment recognition clicked in her mind.

Her composure slipped. "Ian?"

Jake poled forward two steps, checking her out as closely as she was him. "My name's Jake. Ian was my father. That would make me your grandson. May we come in?"

Zabella hesitated so long I thought she might shut and lock the door. Instead she stepped back, gripping the door's edge as if for balance.

She turned inside and we followed. Jake looked around the dim living room. His parents had hidden his origins and told him nothing of the Romani culture. Perhaps he was trying to picture this as the place where his father grew up. His eyes stopped on a John Wayne poster for *The Searchers* that hung above the sideboard where Zabella kept her rum. Two other posters featured the actor in *Rio Bravo* and *True Grit*.

Today she didn't offer tea, dropping heavily into an overstuffed chair. Without being invited, I sat on the couch and Jake followed suit, propping his crutches at an angle against the arm.

The old woman recovered from her shock. I watched the toughness I had learned to expect return to her eyes as she locked her attention on Jake.

"Ian's son," she said.

Jake extracted his wallet and took out a small photo, handing it to her across the coffee table. "Here's my mother and father."

He had not shown this picture to me. But from the look on Zabella's weathered face, the photo removed any doubt about who he was. Her voice grated.

"He never told me he had a son. That was cruel of him."

Jake reached to reclaim the photo. "My father and mother seemed determined to hide their past. I never understood why. But I'm beginning to find out."

Zabella slid a nod in my direction. "What has she told you?"

"As much as she could. I'm hoping you can tell me more. You are my grandmother."

"And you shot him," I said, a bit meanly. "When you were aiming at me. That's what happened to his leg."

A yowl that might have been remorse or a Gypsy curse rose from the old woman's throat. "I did not intend to hit anyone. I wanted to scare you off the mountain."

"Why?" Jake asked.

"She knows."

"Because I discovered the bones of Pesha's first husband," I said, a claim without the benefit of proof unless she confirmed it. "Who killed him, Zabella? Was it you?"

She shook her head and began to keen. I was having none of her crafty bid for sympathy. "Stop moaning and tell us what happened. The sheriff is already investigating his death. You've hidden the truth long enough."

The whining stopped instantly and Zabella's face hardened. "He was an evil man. Pesha was overdramatic, but I understood why she had to get away from that beng."

The same thing Gamma Rose had called Tobar. But that didn't give them the right to kill him.

Did it?

Jake watched her, remarkably detached. "How did it happen?"

Zabella closed her eyes, her mouth puckered. Her head rolled against the flowered cushion.

"What happened?" I demanded again.

She heaved a breath. "Tobar followed them up north. He beat my son and brought Pesha home by force. He drove with her to Gamma Rose's house to retrieve their baby, but no one was home."

She lifted her head and shifted her considerable weight in the chair. "Pesha was clever, and a good actress. She pretended to be sorry for running away and told him that on her mother's property there were ancient symbols that could make them rich."

The petroglyphs the banker had told me about. I'd discounted it as gossip. Were the carvings real?

"Tobar loved money," Zabella went on. "She told him museums had offered Gamma Rose thousands of dollars for each drawing, but Rose would not let them on her land."

When she paused, Jake leaned forward and impaled her with his gaze. "Go on."

Finally she did. "Pesha took him up the mountain, to a cave in that rocky peak. She showed him the drawings, and of course the greedy bastard wanted them. She led him to the top of the rocks to show him a path for getting them safely down. Ian was waiting with my shotgun, his face all bloody and bruised."

"My father killed him?" Jake whispered.

"No." Her head swayed and she smiled. "My Ian was a gentle soul. As much as he loved Pesha, he could not pull the trigger. When she saw that he couldn't, she leaped at Tobar and pushed him off the edge."

I was speechless. Was this true? My grandmother had killed her first husband?

"You're lying," Jake said. "My mother couldn't kill anyone."

Zabella nodded. "She could and she did. Tobar had beat her, raped her. Back then a woman had no remedy. Men treated their wives however they wanted. There were no consequences."

I thought of the tortured eyes in those photos I'd found at the bank. They must have been taken after she married Tobar. I had sensed a threat of violence in her expression, but I would not judge my grandmother. In her shoes I might have done the same thing. I hoped that Jake could forgive her, too.

Yet I wasn't sure I could trust Zabella's story. "How do you know these details? Did Ian tell you?"

She met my eyes and hers were hard as steel. "I was there. I followed him when he came to get the shotgun. That was the last time I saw my son."

In the silence that followed, the scene played through my mind like a silent movie. The only thing I couldn't picture was the cave where they'd found the petroglyphs. Why had I not seen it on two trips up the mountain? It must be well hidden.

"Did Gamma Rose know everything?" I asked.

"Of course. They waited for her and the baby to come home. Pesha wept and told her what happened. Rose was horrified. She called Pesha and Ian murderers and said they did not deserve to raise her grandbaby. She banished them both and said if they ever came back she would turn them in to the police."

This was difficult for me to imagine. But Gamma was much younger then, and she undoubtedly loved the baby she'd been caring for since Pesha left. She told me herself that she'd sent Pesha away.

Still, Ian and Pesha could have easily overpowered my tiny great-grandmother. Why didn't Pesha fight for her baby?

Unless she hated Tobar so much that she didn't want his child.

EIGHTEEN

JAKE AND I sat a full minute in silence. Finally, he rose from the sofa. I followed his lead, ready to leave the strange dark house. He wedged the crutches under his arms and turned toward the door, but Zabella moved swiftly to intercept him.

"Come see me again, Grandson. By yourself."

Jake paused a beat but didn't answer. He propelled himself around her and followed me to the car.

We were quiet as I drove, processing the story we'd just heard. It was hard to accept that his mother, my grandmother, had killed someone. She had good reason to hate Tobar, but she was still guilty of murder.

We might never know if Zabella's version of the story was true. There was no one to confirm or dispute her story.

I stopped in Jake's driveway and killed the engine. He stared through the bug-spotted windshield, making no move to get out.

"Do you believe her?" he said.

I thought a moment. "Most of it. I also think she's capable of lying to cover for herself or her son."

He turned toward me, frowning, and in the turmoil of his eyes I saw a resemblance to the photos of my grandmother. I suddenly remembered Gamma Rose's comment the first day Jake had come to the house. She'd said, "I think we're related," and I passed it off as a symptom of her dementia. But perhaps she had seen a resemblance to her missing daughter.

"I believe the part about my dad not being able to pull the trigger," he said. "Even to save my mother. He had no appetite for violence."

"What about your mother?"

"I don't know. Mom was definitely the dominant force in our family. She could be... volatile sometimes."

"Zabella didn't approve of Pesha, but it was obvious Ian loved her," I said. "Zabella might have pushed Tobar off the edge for the sake of her son's happiness. She once told me she would do anything for him."

Jake sighed and pulled the door handle. "I guess it doesn't make much difference now. Her word is all we have."

He extracted himself from the car, and I adjusted the crutches for his height. He stuck the props under his arms and swung a few steps to test them. "Much better. Thanks."

When he smiled, the resemblance to his mother disappeared. None of the pictures I'd seen of Pesha showed her smiling. I wondered if she ever did.

"Thanks for introducing me to Zabella," he said. "I don't know whether I want any more contact with her, but I hope you and I can keep in touch."

"Absolutely. What will you do now?"

"I'm not sure. I thought about moving back to Missouri. But there's really nothing for me up there. A couple of high school friends, maybe."

"Try for med school again?"

"I think that ship has sailed." He shrugged. "I like my job here okay. What about you? When are you going back home?"

"As soon as the lawyer has Gamma's property settled. I don't think I told you that she left her twenty acres to Zabella."

"Seriously? Why would she do that?"

"To keep the secret of Tobar's death. She made the will years ago."

Jake shook his head. "That land should have gone to you. Especially if there's something valuable up there."

"Zabella's welcome to it. If it were up to me, I wouldn't let anyone remove the petroglyphs any more than Gamma Rose would. They belong where they are. She did leave me the house, but I'm not sure what I'll do with it."

I walked to the driver's side and opened my door. "I'll come by again before I leave. Don't overdo it on that leg."

He gave a mini salute and propelled himself toward the house.

LEAVING JAKE'S PLACE, it dawned on me I'd forgotten to ask Zabella about meeting with the attorney to sign the deed. Dell Sampson's office wasn't far away, so I decided to stop by. Perhaps his assistant could find Zabella's phone number and set up an appointment.

I parked in front of the building and went inside. Dell wasn't in, but his assistant Janelle greeted me.

"Your documents are all ready," she said.

"I neglected to ask Zabella about coming in. Do you think you could find her phone number?"

"She probably has a land line, like your great-grandmother. I have an old phone book around here somewhere."

She found the book and sure enough, there was a listing for Mallosh, Z. She dialed the number and waited through many rings before Zabella answered. I could hear her scratchy voice from where I sat.

Janelle explained who she was and asked if Zabella could come to their office tomorrow.

"I don't drive anymore," she said.

Janelle raised her eyebrows at me.

"I can pick her up," I mouthed.

"Miss Morrell has offered to pick you up," Janelle said. Zabella growled. But if she wanted the land, she had to sign.

She rejected a morning appointment but grudgingly agreed to one-thirty. Before I left, Janelle had me sign the transfer of title for Gamma Rose's home. I was now the owner of two houses, both of them inherited and a far cry from grand.

Next stop was the bank. Now that the attorney had cleared things with the probate judge, I was free to close Gamma Rose's accounts and roll the funds into a new account in my name. There wasn't much left after the funeral. Most of the attorney's fee would come out of my pocket.

My duty to my great-grandmother was winding to a close. As I walked back to my car, a longing for home overcame me. I was more than ready for life to get back to normal. And to make plans with my fiancé. The prospect of getting married amazed me, even more because I still didn't have an answer about my grandmother's length of life.

I sat in the car and instructed the phone-genie to call Drew. In New York it was after five, but he was probably still at work. Sure enough, my call went to voice mail.

"It's nothing important," I told the recording. "Just lonesome. Talk to you soon."

Now that Thelma was retired, she was usually home. So I dialed her number.

The lively voice of my old friend cheered me up immediately. I told her about Drew showing up for the funeral and about discovering the existence of a half-uncle. She was predictably enthusiastic. I held back the news that Drew had proposed so I could tell her that bombshell in person.

"I want all the particulars when you get home," she said. "When are you coming?"

"Day after tomorrow. I can't wait."

Her tone softened. "No answer about your grandmother?"

"Afraid not."

"That's a shame." She sighed. "But sweetie, nobody knows when we wake up in the morning if that day will be our last. We just have to make the most of each day we get."

"Have you been watching Dr. Phil again?" Her round laugh made me smile.

"You'll let me know when you start back?"

"Yes, Mom. I promise."

We signed off. Maybe I could start home after my meeting with Zabella tomorrow instead of waiting another day. Driving at night wouldn't be a problem once I got out of these twisty mountain roads.

The sun had sunk behind those mountains by the time I parked in the dooryard at Gamma's house. Penny and Midnight had already gone to roost.

The chickens! I hadn't made arrangements for Gamma's pets.

What was I going to do with them? If I turned them loose in the woods, they'd be coyote food. I thought of offering them to Zabella, but if she turned them into chicken and dumplings, Gamma Rose would haunt me forever. How the heck did I become the guardian of chickens?

Like Scarlett O'Hara, I would think about that tomorrow. I closed the gate to the chicken pen and went indoors.

The house was stuffy and eerily quiet. I opened the bottle of wine I'd bought when I got Jake's groceries and carried a glass out to the front yard. I sat in the chair where I'd sat with Gamma Rose, and where Drew had proposed, to watch the night descend.

Yellow leaves pirouetted down among black branches. Bird songs faded to silence and tree frogs tuned up. I missed Gamma Rose. I missed Drew and Thelma and Whippoorwill and Bones. Feeling about as lonely as I'd ever been, I sat and listened.

I ROSE AT daylight, fed Penny and Midnight, then sat on the front step with my oatmeal and coffee to watch the sun come up over the mountains. I would miss autumn in the Ozarks, the blended colors, all these trees exhaling oxygen. But not as much as I missed being home.

I was already packed to go. That left the whole morning free before my appointment with Zabella at the attorney's office that afternoon. I couldn't stand to just sit here for five hours, and I felt the need for exercise. I decided on a last hike up behind the house to look for those petroglyphs. This would be my only chance to see them before Zabella owned the land. I wondered if she'd sell the property or raid the cave of its historical treasure.

A cloudbank obstructed the sunrise, but storms here normally rolled in from the west. The clouds should be moving away instead of approaching. I dug sneakers and a sweatshirt out of my suitcase and started the trek.

The uphill path was now familiar. Soon I reached the rocky projection where I'd found the bones. I had not seen a cave on previous visits, but I hadn't explored the back side of the monolithic outcropping. Now I circled its base, craning upward for anything that might be a cavern's mouth. Scrub brush obscured a dark area halfway up the back side of the incline. It might be a cavity in the rocks, but I couldn't tell from down here.

Sunlight broke through the cloudbank and dappled the underbrush. I started climbing. When I got closer, the shadows revealed what was clearly a cave. I quickened my pace.

The effort of ascending left me clammy. By the time I reached the mouth of the cave, clouds blocked the sun again and a chilly breeze curled up from below. I pushed my sunglasses on top of my head and peered through an opening barely taller than my head. The hollow area appeared only about ten feet deep. It was too dark inside to see any drawings on the walls, so I switched on my phone's flashlight and ducked inside.

Nothing interesting on the cave walls here, but a passageway disappeared in the shadows to my left. I shined my light toward it and followed the curve, stooping to avoid the rocky ceiling.

The passage opened to an area where the air was cooler and smelled like turned earth. The ceiling rose enough that I was able to stand up. I scanned the walls with the light, moving deeper into the cave.

At first glimpse I wasn't sure what I was seeing. Then the rudimentary outline of a deer took shape. Eureka, I whispered, feeling like a real explorer. I held the light closer and examined the shallow carving. Its outlines were stained black, perhaps with charcoal or ashes from a fire. Another drawing looked feline, possibly a cougar. There was a snake with a forked tongue and a larger animal with heavy shoulders and short, curved horns that resembled a bison.

My heartbeat skittered. The carvings were breathtaking and unblemished by time. No wonder natural history buffs and paleontologists would covet them. The cave felt imbued with the spirit of the artist who carved these images, hundreds of years before I was born.

The flash on my phone's camera bounced off the stone walls like an explosion. Drew would have loved to see these treasures, but at least he could see the photos.

I played my flashlight over the opposite wall in search of more drawings. Something on the cave floor caught my eye—a mound next to the wall below a shelf of rock. The light-colored mass looked like fabric. I moved closer and realized it was a sleeping bag and pillow. Nearby were the remains of a campfire.

My shoulder blades prickled. "Holy Roller," I whispered, suddenly wishing Sheriff Donovan were here. These items were definitely not stone-age. Someone had been staying here recently.

The camp felt transient rather than permanent, with no food or water in evidence. I thought of the breach in the fence near Zabella's house. Someone could come and go at that spot without being seen. Why would anyone camp here? Maybe a homeless person, or teenagers looking for an adventure. Or someone running from the law.

A sound from the cave opening froze me in place. I hid the phone's light against my leg and listened, my heartbeat in my throat.

Footsteps. Unmistakable, and getting closer.

This was not an animal walking on padded feet. These steps were human, which was scarier than any critter. I stood as still as I could, staring toward the cave's opening while my skin twitched and crawled.

A figure appeared, silhouetted against the faint light. I saw a corona of unruly hair, an unidentifiable body shape, and two legs.

There was nowhere to hide, so I took the offensive. "Who's there?" I shouted. "Who are you?"

The figure stopped short, then came closer, moving like something ancient. In the faint luminosity from the entrance, I made out a loose cape that covered the person's body, but I could not distinguish whether it was male or female. Its shape loomed like a monster from a childhood nightmare.

"Who are you?" I said again.

A noise like a snort. "None of your business. Who are you?"

The voice was coarse but definitely female. She was very tall.

"I'm Chantalene."

She waved her arms, her tone unhinged. "Mulo! You are a mulo from the other side!"

Mulo was one of the Romani words I knew—evil spirit. The woman was a Gypsy.

Comprehension spread through me, thick and liquid. Could it be? The anonymous roses at the funeral, the missing will, the mysterious visitor in the night.

"Pesha?" I said. My voice wobbled.

Her arms stopped in midair. She shrieked. "Mulo!"

In a quick movement that took me by surprise, she grabbed a piece of wood from the cave floor and held it like a club. One end was wrapped in cloth like a medieval torch. A growl came from her throat. Her aura glowed deep red, so dark I could barely see it.

I lifted my arm, palm out, and talked fast. "I'm not an evil spirit. I am the great-granddaughter of Gamma Rose. My mother was LaVita."

She flinched and weaved on her feet. I stepped forward and reached to catch her, but she righted herself and pulled away. I wondered if she saw the resemblance to my mother that others had seen, then remembered she wouldn't know what her daughter looked like. She'd only seen her as a baby.

She steadied herself against the rock wall. I couldn't see her eyes, but her hands were hooked like claws. If she attacked, I'd be in for a serious battle.

"LaVita," she said, a harsh whisper. "What happened to her?"

"She's dead. She was murdered. Like her father, Tobar."

A wail. "Our family is cursed."

"I don't believe in curses. LaVita's death had nothing to do with what happened here."

"Tobar has cursed us! We will come to a violent end."

I wasn't buying the melodrama. "Your son Jake is alive and healthy. Why did you abandon him? He thinks you're dead."

"I am dead. I died when I lost Ian."

My face flamed. "Your son doesn't matter? Or the fact that you have a granddaughter?"

"I have no granddaughter."

"You do," I insisted. "I am LaVita's daughter, your granddaughter."

"You're trying to trick me. You are a mulo!" Her arms waved crazily. "Tobar sent you to get his revenge."

I shined my light toward her then. She jerked her head away but I had seen the face of my grandmother. Her coarse black hair was streaked with gray and hung in mats past her shoulders. Her face was a maze of lines. She had not lived in this cave all these years. Where had she been? I no longer doubted the unraveling of her rational mind.

She looked as old as Zabella, though she would be two decades younger. In her sixties, and still alive. Like Gamma Rose, she had defied the mitochondrial disorder, if she ever had it.

My eyes watered. I wanted to thank her for living. To tell her that she'd given me back my life, that I wanted to know her. I couldn't speak past the lump in my throat. Even if I could explain, I felt sure she wouldn't understand or care.

I backed against the cave wall. She was blocking the exit and I had no weapon, nor any wish to harm her. All I had was words.

"Grandmother Pesha," I said in the gentlest voice I could manage. "Let me take you to Jake. He's right here in town, and he misses you."

She didn't move, so I took a step forward. "He hurt his leg. He's in a cast from his hip to his toes and needs your help." If I thought this would engender a maternal instinct in her, I'd forgotten whom I was dealing with. This woman had abandoned both her children.

I changed tactics. "The sheriff has identified Tobar's bones." Not quite true, but close enough. "Zabella told us you killed him. I know he mistreated you. Come with me to see Jake, I won't report you to police."

"Zabella!" she screeched. The whites of her eyes twitched in the dim light. "That evil witch always hated me!"

"I know. Did she lie about Tobar? Is she the one who pushed him?"

Her head began a creepy gyration, as if she heard voices from somewhere else.

"If Zabella killed him," I said, "don't let her get away with accusing you. I can get her arrested. The sheriff is a friend of mine." Not exactly true, but I was throwing out everything I could think of.

Suddenly she stopped, eyeing me, then turned and scuttled out of the cave. The move was as agile and quick as someone half her age.

Taken aback, I took a few seconds to follow. When I exited the mouth of the cave, she was gone. I scanned the slope below, seeing nothing.

Stones rattled down from above and I stepped back and looked up. Rain spattered my face. Pesha was scaling the cliff like a mountain goat. The sight petrified me. I expected her to plummet at any moment. The wind had picked up and was slashing rain against the slick rocks.

She kept climbing. Every instinct told me to let her go. But now that I'd found my grandmother, I didn't want to lose her. If Jake and I could get her some help, perhaps her sanity could be restored. And if she fell, how could I tell Jake I didn't even try to stop her?

I began to climb. The steep slope wasn't vertical, but it felt like it. I grabbed onto scrub brush and found footholds that flaked terrifyingly beneath my feet. How was she able to do this at her age? Perhaps she was too senseless to comprehend the danger. I understood quite well that if I slipped, my body would crash onto rocky points that meant broken bones or death.

I kept going but Pesha climbed faster, taking crazy risks. Pebbles and rain peppered down on my head. Her foot slipped and sent a basketball-sized boulder rolling past my ear. I closed my eyes and hung on.

Finally, she reached the top and disappeared from sight. I scrambled to catch up, terrified that when I periscoped over the lip of the plateau, she'd be waiting to smash in my skull.

Slowly, slowly, I peeked over the edge. Wet hair hung in my face.

Pesha was standing on the far side of the cliff, facing the precipice where I'd found Tobar's bones. Rain plastered the cape around her body.

"Pesha! Stop! Talk to me. Let me help you."

I belly-crawled onto the flat rock surface and painfully pushed to my feet. "Wait, please." I was afraid to move closer. "Please turn around and look at me."

Instead, she moved closer to the ledge where Tobar had gone over.

"Please," I begged. "Just stop a minute. I'm not going to hurt you. Please look at me."

But she didn't. She took two quick steps and leaped into the rain, dropping into the chasm like a winged stone.

NINETEEN

"NOOOOOOO!" My scream died in the wind. I braced for the awful sound of human bones breaking on rocks, but all I heard was rain and a distant rumble of thunder.

I dropped on hands and feet and crawled toward the place where Pesha disappeared, not wanting to look. Yet, if there was a chance she'd survived the fall, I had to know. Hugging the rounded edge of the plateau, I peered over.

The clouded skies didn't cast much light into the rift. I squinted and wiped wet hair from my face. At first I saw nothing. Then my eyes registered something that looked like cloth caught on a jagged rock. Pesha's cape. Above it, a smear of red.

I leaned out farther. An updraft brushed my face but the fabric didn't move, as if weighted by something heavy. I inched sideways for a better perspective.

Pesha hung by one arm that was caught in the cape. The unnatural angle of her shoulder sent a surge of nausea through my stomach and flattened me to the cliff's edge. When the urge to retch abated, I looked again. Her bloodied head hung sideways. One hip was wedged against the limestone rock face. I couldn't tell if she was breathing.

I inched away from the brink and stood, fumbling for my cell phone. By some miracle, it hadn't fallen from my back pocket during the climb. Shielding the phone from the rain, I checked for reception. No service. Carefully I crossed the plateau, watching the screen. When a single bar appeared, I froze in that spot and pushed the number for Sheriff Donovan's cell.

It went to voicemail. Profanities echoed from the hills.

"Bring the recovery team," I yelled into the phone. "Hurry! Someone went off the cliff behind Gamma Rose's house—again." Then as an afterthought. "This is Chantalene."

When I looked at the screen, it was black. Did the message record? My battery was almost gone.

I shook the phone and the lone bar showed up again. The sheriff's office number was still in my call log. I tapped the number and was grateful to hear the voice of the female officer I'd met before. She promised to send help immediately.

I sat on the ground to wait and closed my eyes. My ears were ringing and my hair hung in sodden hunks. I wrapped my arms around my knees and put my head down, rocking, shivering in my waterlogged jacket.

As suddenly as it had started, the rain stopped. I watched it move across the hillside with brown leaves falling in its wake. Sunlight knifed between retreating clouds and spotlighted the ridge where I sat.

There was no sound from the chasm and I couldn't look again.

I lifted my face to the sun and closed my eyes. One disconnected thought after another leapfrogged in my head. My grandmother alive... a reprieve... tell Drew... probably dead now... definitely crazy... Jake! Tell Jake! ...the funeral flowers, the dark SUV in the night... Pesha? ...recovery team... how much longer?

On and on it went, while I held myself like a child and the minutes seemed endless.

Nearly an hour later, I heard the sheriff and his team thrashing up the hill. They brought ropes and pitons, medical supplies and a stretcher.

By then I was shaking. The sheriff took off his coat and wrapped it around my shoulders. "Same place?" he asked, and I nodded. "Jesus."

He and the Masons went to work. I rested my forehead on my knees and stared at the wet ground without the strength to stand. When they brought up her flaccid body, I knew she was dead. The sheriff said they would take her to the hospital anyway. We made our laborious way down the mountain through dripping brush to the waiting ambulance.

"I'll get your statement later," the sheriff said when I gave him back his coat. "Go indoors and get warm." They loaded the body and left.

Inside the cabin, I sat in a hot bath with steam clouding around me. I didn't feel the heat. I couldn't feel anything. The encounter with Pesha was like a barely remembered nightmare. If I closed my eyes tightly, I could almost believe it wasn't real.

My skin was red and rippled when I finally stopped shaking and got out of the tub. I toweled dry and looked at the clock. It felt like two days since I'd left the house this morning, but it had been only a few hours. My mind wasn't processing well. All I could think was that I had to pick up Zabella by one-thirty. The title to Gamma's land had to be resolved before I could go home.

Zombie-like, I dressed, found my keys, and plugged my phone into the car charger. My mind was still foggy when I tapped the horn in Zabella's front yard. She came out of the house slowly and wedged herself into the passenger seat, grunting as she propped the tiger-headed cane between us by the console. I said nothing nor offered to help. Zabella was never a friend to Pesha, and I felt no obligation to tell her anything.

We rode in silence for several miles before she spoke. "I saw the ambulance. More trouble on that mountain."

The grating voice raked down my spine. I tightened my jaw and didn't answer.

"Another body?"

I glanced at her then, keeping my face blank. Her jet eyes glittered, hard and faceted. I saw an intelligence there that I had overlooked. "What makes you say that?"

She shrugged. "Why else would an ambulance show up? And the sheriff."

No vehicle that traveled past her house escaped those cagey eyes. I pictured her using over-sized binoculars.

Her tone softened. "Was it Pesha?"

I stopped the car in the road and turned on her, frowning.

"I never believed she was dead," Zabella said. "I felt her presence."

"Horseshit."

"When Ian died, word reached me eventually. If Pesha was dead, I would have heard. I would have told Gamma Rose."

"And yet you didn't know about Jake."

We stared at each other for a long moment. Then I lifted my foot from the brake and drove on.

I let another mile pass. "She threw herself off the ledge in the same place where Tobar died."

Zabella nodded and watched the road.

AT THE ATTORNEY'S office, Janelle explained the legal description on the documents that would transfer the title of Gamma's acres. It had been surveyed when she and Yoors bought the property and we agreed to accept that document, which was included in the abstract. Zabella and I signed where directed. Our business was finished in fifteen minutes and I rose to leave.

I thanked Janelle and spoke to Zabella. "I'll drive you home now."

Zabella stayed put, ignoring me. "How long before the deed is registered in the county records?" she asked Janelle.

"I'll hand-deliver it to the courthouse this afternoon."

"Good," Zabella said. "As soon as it's filed, draw up a deed transferring the acreage from me to my grandson, Jake Mallosh. Let me know when this is done. I will sign and pay your fee."

I sat back down. "What?"

She placed both hands on the tiger-head of her cane and said nothing.

Finally I said, "His last name is Wayne."

"Put both names then. But his real name is Mallosh."

Using the cane for leverage, she rose and shambled out of the office. Janelle and I exchanged surprised looks before I followed the old woman to my car.

Once we were on the road, I glanced over at her. "That's a nice thing you're doing for Jake."

"He is also Gamma Rose's grandson. You got the house. Jake should get something."

"Something besides shot in the leg?"

She waved the gibe away. "It was a ricochet."

"I thought you'd want to keep the land just to spite me."

She scowled. "I despised Pesha for taking my son. Nothing to do with you. You took care of Gamma Rose. And you brought me my grandson."

I chewed on that for a while. The only access to the land was from Gamma Rose's house, which I owned, or through Zabella's land to the east. I began to see her strategy.

"Maybe he will build a house there," she said.

I was pretty sure that would never happen. But who was I to quash an old woman's dream.

I DELIVERED ZABELLA to her house, then turned around and drove back to town. There was one more unpleasant task I must do before word got around.

The visiting nurse was finishing up Jake's first physical therapy session when I arrived. His face was white, his jaw clenching, but he made no sound nor did he complain. I knew from experience that PT can feel like torture. It also works wonders if you do it faithfully.

After the nurse left, Jake pushed back in his recliner. His hairline was damp. I could tell he was hurting, but he smiled.

"I'm glad you stopped by. I thought you were going back to Oklahoma today."

"There's been a complication." I took a seat on the sofa and stared at my hands for a moment before I could meet his eyes. "I have news about your mother."

He lifted his head. "Really?"

"I went up the mountain looking for those petroglyphs and found that she'd been camping in a cave up there."

He frowned. "In a cave? That's crazy. Why would you think it was her?"

"I saw her."

He looked at me a full five seconds. "Are you sure?"

"Yes."

"She's alive?"

"Not exactly."

Sparing him the worst details, I told him what had happened. "She wasn't in her right mind, Jake. She thought I was an evil spirit. She threw herself off the cliff in the exact spot where Tobar died."

Jake stared at the opposite wall, faintly shaking his head.

"The guilt must have eaten at her for years," I said. "Maybe her conscience eroded her sanity."

This was a generous view of the wild woman I'd encountered. I wasn't sure she had a conscience, but it might be something Jake needed to believe. We make excuses for our parents, just as they make excuses for us.

"I told Sheriff Donovan she was your mother. He'll be calling you soon."

Jake nodded. His expression was blank.

"You okay?"

"I will be. I thought she was already dead, so this isn't the shock it might have been." He heaved a deep breath. "I'm pissed that she never came back. I was just a kid, and she didn't even care what happened to me."

"We can't know that. Her mind was messed up."

"It started when Dad died. I guess it got worse and worse."

Pesha said that she died when Ian died. She'd also killed someone to be with him, and left two children because of him. That was more than love. That was obsession.

In the photographs I'd found at the bank, her eyes looked spooky. She was only a teenager then. I suspected Pesha's mental problems started earlier than anyone knew. Maybe the day she saw her father die.

Sheriff Donovan called Jake while I was there. Pesha had been pronounced dead on arrival at the hospital. He needed Jake to identify the body and specify a funeral home.

I was to report to the sheriff's office at nine the next morning and give my statement.

Jake and I drove to the hospital where he'd been released two days ago. They had cleaned up his mother as best they could and laid her on a gurney in the pathology department. Jake was dry-eyed when he confirmed it was indeed his mother. At my suggestion, he called the same funeral home that managed Gamma Rose's service.

There would be no Gypsy caravan for Pesha, no mourners or raft of flowers. "She's to be cremated," he told them. "No funeral."

I dropped Jake back at his house. He looked wrung out. I left him alone so he could rest.

Before leaving cell-phone range, I phoned Drew and Thelma and filled them in. The day's events had taken away my excitement for the trip home. I dreaded the long drive alone with too much time to think. Drew and Thelma, though, latched on to the positive news. If both Pesha and Gamma Rose had lived to advanced years, so could I.

Driving back to the little house in the woods, I made up my mind to sell the place. It didn't feel charming anymore. It felt creepy. On Gamma's land line, I called Dell Sampson's sister-in-law, the realtor he'd recommended. She agreed to list the property but was dubious about a quick sale.

"I expect it will need some updating," she said.

"For sure. But I can't afford that. I need to sell it as is."

I told her I'd leave a key under the concrete chicken by the front door, and the old car under the trees went with the house. I had no idea if it would run.

DARKNESS GATHERED IN the woods. I sat outdoors, replaying everything that had happened in the last weeks, from the day I found Gamma Rose in the hospice facility, to the day she died, and the wild incident with Pesha on the mountain. It seemed like a weird old movie, something I'd watched but didn't quite believe.

The owl called from the woods, lonely and haunting. Nobody here but me and the Gypsy mulés that roamed the hills. Goosebumps shimmered across my shoulder blades.

I went in the house and called Uncle Jake. "Could I crash on your sofa tonight?"

"I'd be glad for the company," he said. "I'm feeling pretty bummed, myself. We both lost the last of our family today. Except for each other."

He still had a grandmother, but I didn't point that out. He wasn't quite ready to claim Zabella, which I could understand. I would not mention her gift of the land. That was her news to tell, not mine.

I tossed a few things in my tote bag and made my third trip of the day to Madison. That narrow, twisty road was getting wearisome. At least I'd already be in town for tomorrow morning's appointment with the sheriff, no more than five minutes from Jake's house.

That evening, over take-out from the Good Eats Café, Jake and I traced what we knew of our weird ancestors. I sketched a family tree on the take-out sack. We dredged up any good memories we could recall, and we drank a few beers. Near ten o'clock, I rolled up in a blanket on his faux-leather couch and slept without dreaming.

A CRYSTALLINE MORNING followed yesterday's rain. It felt like a good omen.

I met Sheriff Donovan in his office and gave him the long version of how I met my grandmother. He recorded our conversation on a cassette machine circa 1995.

I'd told him earlier about the vehicle that appeared at Gamma's house in the night. He said they would search the woods close to Zabella's house. I speculated that Pesha was responsible for the theft of Gamma's will and the unexplained flowers at her funeral. I had no idea how long she'd been camping on the ridge, or where she'd been the years before that. Jake might want to trace her past, but I simply didn't care.

The sheriff scratched his stubbly jaw and asked a few questions but basically let me talk. I detailed the tumultuous history of Jake's and my families, including that Pesha supposedly had pushed Tobar to his death.

"Zabella said she was there when it happened. She might have pushed him herself, for all I know. But Pesha had a stronger motive, and there's no one to dispute the claim."

"I'll interview Missus Mallosh about the bones," he said. "But I doubt her story will change."

He clicked off the recorder, and I paused. "So am I free to leave town?"

"I'll give you a call tomorrow morning. We're collecting evidence from the cave and I might have questions about what we find. But after talking with both you and Jake, I'm satisfied his mother's death was a suicide." He shoved a notepad across the desk. "Write down your name, home address, phone, and email."

I complied and said goodbye to Sheriff Donovan for what I hoped was the last time. Then I drove down Main Street and parked between Walgreens and the Tractor Supply store to pick up supplies for the road home.

TWENTY

TRUE TO HIS word, Sheriff Donovan phoned at midmorning. "We found a beat-up SUV hidden in the trees between the Mallosh house and yours," he said. "Missouri plates, out of date. It looked like she'd been living in her car for quite a while. Your great-grandmother's will was on the front seat."

"That solves the last mystery, I guess."

I wondered if it registered in Pesha's mind that she'd been left out of her mother's will. What if she had returned home hoping to reconcile with Gamma Rose? If my car hadn't been parked in the yard, maybe she would have knocked on the door instead of driving away. Who knew what was going through her disheveled mind.

"I'll mail the will to you when we close the case," the sheriff said. "You're cleared to leave town anytime you want. Drive safe."

"I will. Thanks for all your help. You can give the will to Jake instead. I've turned over the executor chores to him. He's actually a closer relative than I am."

I felt Gamma Rose with me as I attended to last minute details around the house. We had made a few memories here, and I was grateful for those. Finally, I said goodbye to the place, locked it up, and hit the road.

FIVE HOURS LATER, I turned onto the road that led to my clapboard farmhouse in the Kiamichi hills. Lost in my thoughts, I barely remembered the drive.

The sun knelt on the horizon and a banner of violet light welcomed me home. People think of Key West or Hawaii for beautiful sunsets, but Oklahoma's are often spectacular. Part of that comes from dramatic cloud formations. The rest is a product of perpetual dust and pollen in the air. Irritants with silver linings.

Thelma's little coupe was parked in front of my house. I had phoned to let her know approximately when I'd be arriving. The silhouette of her stout form in the corral, pouring oats into Whippoorwill's feed pan, made me smile. When she heard me drive in, she straightened up and waved like a beauty queen.

Bones recognized the car and ran to greet me. She barked and leaped beside the door until I got out. I knelt on the dirt to hug her and accept doggie kisses.

"How's my good girl? I missed you."

She was even more excited when I opened the back of the SUV and unloaded a wire cage containing Penny and Midnight.

"You, with chickens?" Thelma asked, giving me a robust hug. "Will wonders never cease."

I shrugged. "I couldn't just leave them."

The chickens did not share Bones's joy. She bounced around the cage, wagging and whining, while they squawked and beat their wings against the wire until I feared for their lives.

"We better put them in the barn," Thelma said. "Can chickens have heart attacks?"

Since I'd had no intention of housing chickens, ever, I had no pen for them. Until I got one built, they would have to be confined. I carried the crate to the barn and Thelma followed with a bucket of water. I brought in the chicken feed I'd bought in Madison and poured some into a shallow pan.

Thelma poured the water into a trough. "These are good lookin' hens."

"Humph."

Left outside, Bones huffed and whined and stuck her snout between two boards. But she couldn't get in, and I was pretty sure the birds couldn't get out. If they did, they were on their own.

When we came out of the barn, Whippoorwill whinnied and leaned over the top rail of the corral, pricking his ears forward. I hugged his neck and scratched under his forelock, cooing to him in the way my dad had taught me to speak to a horse. Whip tossed his head and nuzzled me with scratchy lips.

God, it was good to be home.

By now dusk had descended. "Want me to help you unload?" Thelma said.

"I think I'll just grab my bag and leave the rest until daylight. Come on in."

Thelma had brought a Mexican casserole for our supper. She was a great cook and an even better friend.

With our stocking feet on the coffee table and short glasses of bourbon-and-seven in our hands, we talked a long time. Bones curled up on the sofa with her head on my lap, and I swear she was smiling. All was right with her world once again.

Thelma wanted every detail about my great-grandmother, Uncle Jake, the house I'd inherited, and my crazy grandma. It was cathartic for me to tell the stories, and I took my time. Finding words for my strange family history helped me untangle my emotions. Sometimes I don't know how I feel until I say it out loud. Thelma's questions helped me see things through someone else's eyes.

Finally, I came to the best part. "Drew asked me to marry him."

"You buried the lede!" she hollered. "Did you say yes?"

I paused a bit just to tease her, then grinned. "I did. I guess we're engaged."

She sprang from her chair and smothered me with a hug. "I'm so happy for you! You guys were meant to be together. It's too bad it took you so long."

"I'm supposed to travel to New York next month."

"That's exciting! Are you going to be married up there?"

"No. Well, I don't know. We haven't made plans yet." Sitting with Thelma, I'd changed my mind about a wedding on some tropical island. "If he doesn't mind, I'd like to be married here. So you can be my matron of honor."

Thelma's trademark laughter rang through the house. It sounded like a baby's belly laugh on a megaphone. Bones lifted her head and stared.

"I don't know about the honor part," she said, "but I'm definitely a matron. Isn't there some age limit on that job?" She drained her glass and glanced at the clock. "Lands, it's almost eleven and you've got to be tired from the drive. I better go home."

I walked out on the porch with her. There was a Halloween moon above the barn and a breeze that felt more like spring than fall. She tooted her horn as she drove away.

Watching her taillights recede into the night, I stood a moment breathing the soft air. I wondered how Jake's physical therapy was going. Whether Zabella told him she was deeding Gamma's property to him in the hope that he would stay. And whether he would allow the petroglyphs to be removed from the mountain. Something in me felt unsettled, as if I had forsaken my Gypsy heritage, or left unfinished business.

Drew's ringtone warbled from inside the house, jolting me out of my brooding. I ran to answer.

We talked for a while, but it was already midnight on the East Coast and we were both yawning. He signed off with the promise to call earlier the next evening. I filled Bones's dogfood bowl and hit the shower.

What is it about being naked in streaming water that so often steams open the brain? With hot needles pounding the stiffness from my shoulders, an idea occurred to me. Something that might make me feel better about the loss of Gamma Rose. But I was too tired to make decisions, and I couldn't wait to sleep in my own bed.

THE NEXT MORNING I fed the animals, cleaned the dust from the house, and dumped a bag of laundry into the washer. Hammered nails in a loose board on the corral. Ordered chicken wire and steel posts delivered from a farm supply store in town. I would buy a pre-fab mini-shed to use for a chicken house, though the operation would put a crimp in my budget. Luckily the man I planned to marry was a prosperous lawyer.

I phoned the tag agency to make sure I still had a job. Fortunately, they wanted me back. Unfortunately, they wanted me there tomorrow.

That afternoon I called Jake. He had just finished his therapy and sounded winded.

"Glad you made it home safe," he said. "How are things down on the farm?"

He made it sound fun, like Old MacDonald's. Maybe that's how he pictured it if he'd never spent time on a farm before. Except for the near poverty, maybe that picture wasn't so far off.

"It's good," I told him. "Really glad to be here. How's the leg?"

"Getting better. Doesn't hurt so much to walk today. But I'm already wanting to get this cast off. It itches inside and I can't scratch it."

I laughed, knowing the feeling. "Use the handle of a fly swatter," I told him. "Listen, did Zabella tell you she's giving Gamma Rose's twenty acres to you?"

"She did. Somehow she wangled my phone number and asked me to stop by her house. First I said no, but she played the grandmother card. The woman sure knows how to work people."

"Indeed."

"It feels strange, though. I have no idea what to do with the property."

"Here's an idea. If you have any interest in staying in Arkansas, I'd like to deed Gamma Rose's house to you, as well."

"What? Why would you do that?"

"I have no sentimental attachment to the house. I contacted a real estate agent about putting it on the market, and she said it probably won't sell without a lot of work. If you would actually live there, I'd rather give it to you. You could fix it up to suit yourself, and we would be keeping Gamma Rose's property all together."

Silence on the line.

"Jake?"

"I can't take your inheritance."

"I'd rather you own the house than strangers. She was your grandmother."

Another pause. "I need to give it some thought."

"Take all the time you need. No pressure. And be kind to that bum leg."

"Thanks, Chantalene. You're the best niece I ever had."

"I definitely am." We were laughing when I hung up the phone.

DREW CALLED THAT evening. We talked for an hour about the fun things we could do when I visited New York. Some of them in his apartment bedroom. I told him that I'd offered Gamma Rose's house to Jake, and he liked the idea.

"But if he decides against it," he said, "I could hire a contractor to fix up the place so it would sell."

We decided to think about that another time.

He had let the private detective go, since Pesha was no longer missing.

"I want you to cancel my appointment with that specialist, too," I told him.

"Why? He might have updated information. I read about an experimental drug that might grow new mitochondria—"

"I don't want to know. Pesha and Gamma Rose outlasted the defect, and that's enough for me. I want to live one day at a time and not obsess about what's coming."

"Who is this I'm talking to?"

I smiled. "I'm going to savor each moment like a yogi."

"Wow. That's heavy."

"Are you making fun of me?"

"Only a little. I think it sounds great. I've invested so much time trying to advance my career that I'm missing out on the present. I don't want that to happen now that we're together."

"I just love the heck out of you."

"I know." I could hear him smile. "But are you positive about the doctor's appointment?"

"I am."

"Then that's what we'll do."

We said goodbye feeling happy and horny.

That evening as I brushed my teeth before bed, I felt a strange tingling in my mouth. I rinsed and spat, then leaned toward the mirror and opened wide.

At first I didn't see anything, but it tingled again and I looked closer. On the left side, a smooth shape like a kidney bean was rising on my tongue. I blinked. My eyebrows shot up.

"Holly Roller," I said, and heard the faint echo of Gamma Rose's cackle.

Marcia Preston writes mysteries and women's literary fiction. Her second mystery, *Song of the Bones*, won the Mary Higgins Clark Award for suspense fiction and the Oklahoma Book Award. She lives beside a creek in central Oklahoma, where she feeds the birds and dodges tornadoes.